Callie and the Cult

Barbara Ann Philleo

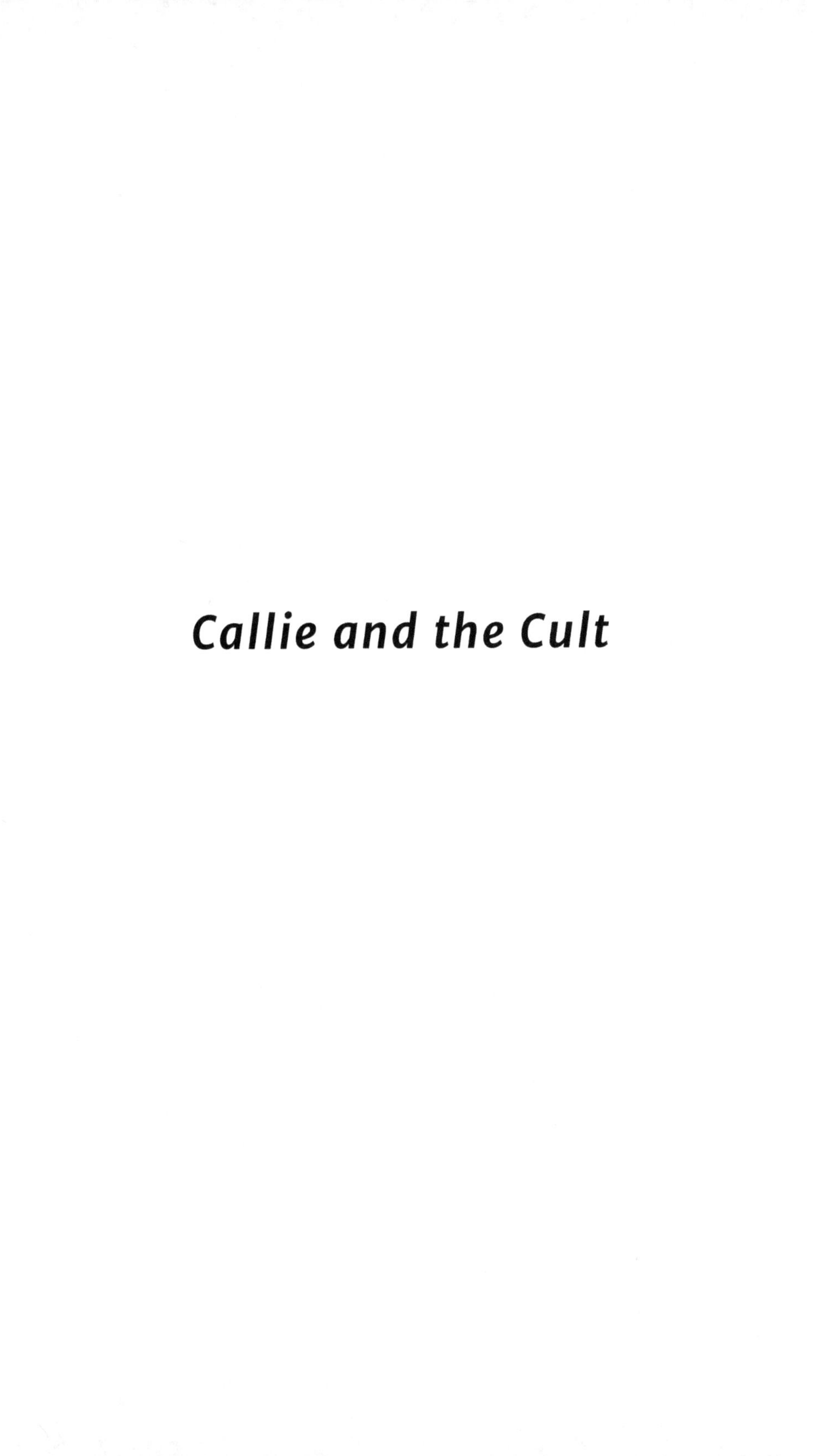

Callie and the Cult

Other books by Barbara Ann Philleo

CANDLECURSE:
The Adventures of Molly Wiggins and Taco

MONSTER MOUNTAIN MYSTERY:
The Adventures of Molly Wiggins and Taco

PARTNERS IN CRIME:
The Adventures of Molly Wiggins and Taco

STICKS and STONES

THE HEAVEN CLUB

Callie and the Cult

Available on Amazon.com
Reviews are always welcome

DEDICATION

This book is lovingly dedicated to the memory of
Thomas A. Philleo, father of my children

CHAPTER ONE

"Stop! Thief!" screamed a white-haired lady who'd witnessed a young man with a laptop under his arm run out the door of the discount store. Callie Morris and Sarah Jo Foster looked on incredulously as the manager as well as several employees, donned in their red vests, flew out the door in pursuit. The service desk manager had called 911 and soon the authorities were in the parking lot with the thief in custody.

"Can you believe this, Sarah Jo?" asked Callie. "I mean we just came here to find shoes for the dance."

"Well, it looks like we got more than just shoes," said Sarah Jo, as she clutched her pair tighter. "I guess this will do it for excitement for me today."

"Yeh, no kidding," replied Callie. "It's not even safe to go shopping these days."

"Well, don't let out your breath yet. Pastor Martin says this is just the beginning – lawlessness, as he puts it," said Sarah Jo.

"I know, but he also says that God will protect us," Callie reminded her friend.

Callie was sure glad that her best friend, Sarah Jo, had moved back to Pine Moor. She'd had to live without her for too long during the time Sarah Jo and her family had been in Addison. In the meantime, she'd made other friends but none so close as Sarah Jo. From the time they met in Sunday school as little girls, they hit it off. Practically inseparable, the two became like sisters, thought Callie. Since she herself was an only child, it made sense that Sarah Jo would fill that void. Of course Sarah Jo had her brother Mark, but you can't play dolls with a kid brother. Now that they were older, well into their teens, there were other things to think about. For one thing, she and Sarah Jo had both come to the Lord and accepted Him as their Lord and Saviour. And then there were boys, well, maybe not for Sarah Jo. She, on the other hand, was not at all displeased that God had made two genders that were so different. Of course, guys could be a real pain – even jerks, but they still had her interest.

So tonight was the big dance sponsored by several local churches that believed supervised interaction of a mixed group of teens was better than individual dating. Callie thought it would be fun, but scary. She and Sarah Jo would be riding together with Mrs. Foster. It would be held in Fellowship Hall of the largest of the churches, Beacon Community Church. Callie hoped that Donnie Maxwell would be there, but she didn't say anything to Sarah Jo about it. No need to make a big deal of it.

"Callie," called Mom from the kitchen, "can you help me for just a second?"

"All right...coming." Mom was at the sink with water up to her elbows washing carrots from the garden.

"Will you pull up my sleeves a little higher? I think I got ahead of myself here. I've got to scrub these carrots really well before I can them." Callie performed the requested task. "Thanks, dear." Callie snatched a carrot out of the water and munched on it.

"Hey, these are good," declared Callie. "Really sweet."

"I might need some help later, Callie, so please don't wander off," said her mother.

"Wander off? Sounds like I'm a little kid."

"Well, you know what I mean. I know you've got the dance tonight, but I'll only need you for awhile this afternoon. What are you wearing to the dance?" asked Mom.

"I don't know, but there's a dress code as in girls have to wear a dress or a skirt and blouse or something. They never have to do that at public school. They wear what they want – jeans and a top, that kind of thing," answered Callie.

"Yes, that's the difference between society's ways and God's ways. If there was no difference, then no one would notice."

"Anyway, I'll probably wear that midnight blue dress with the diagonal stripes across the top," said Callie.

"Good choice," answered Mom.

"I think I'll call Sarah Jo and see what her mother said about what happened at the store today. I'll bet she had a fit. She probably won't let us go shopping anymore," sighed Callie.

"Don't be judgmental, honey. That could've been a very dangerous situation, especially when someone's desperate enough to go out in broad daylight and steal a high ticket item," said Mom. Callie disappeared into the family room with the cordless phone and punched in Sarah Jo's number.

"Hey Mark, is Sarah Jo there? Oh, you heard, huh? Well, we were in no danger. Just go get your sister, okay?" Callie heard the phone clunk, then a yell for Sarah Jo.

"Hey Callie, what's up?" Sarah Jo sounded breathless.

"Just wondering what your mom said when you told her about what happened at SmartMart this morning."

"Well, she said it didn't surprise her; just that it seemed odd to have happened in a small town like Pine Moor," answered Sarah Jo.

"I spose," said Callie, "but maybe that's why the guy tried it; cuz no one would expect it to happen."

"Could be," said Sarah Jo. "How do your shoes look with the dress you're wearing – do they match it?"

"Yep, as good as what I figured. I'm glad I didn't take the other ones. They would've looked dumb," declared Callie.

"Are you excited about going?" wondered Sarah Jo.

"I guess so. It could be fun. Well, except if Riley Woodboro asks me to dance. If he steps on my foot, it'll be flat as a pancake - goodbye shoe!"

"Aw, he's not so bad," said Sara Joe. "He's a big guy, but he's a *nice* big guy."

Callie chuckled. "If you say so."

*****

That evening, Mrs. Foster dropped the girls off in front of the church and reminded them that she would be back promptly at ten o'clock.

"If I'm not right in front here, you wait for me but don't leave the front of the church," advised Sarah Jo's mother." The girls nodded simultaneously. As Mrs. Foster drove off, the girls entered the building and went downstairs to Fellowship Hall. A crowd of young people some of whom Callie and Sarah Jo knew – the ones from their church anyway - filled the hall. The boys were lined up on one side, the girls on the other.

"Wow, this is going to be a blast – not!" said Callie as she and Sarah Jo made their way over to the refreshment table.

"At least the food looks good," observed Sarah Jo as she took an oatmeal cookie from a doilied plate.

"Ladies and gentlemen," announced Pastor Martin. "I can see that no one wants to get out on the dance floor so my lovely wife and I will do the honors. Please find a partner and feel free to join in at any time. Pastor Martin gathered his wife into his arms and ceremoniously began to waltz across the floor. They set an example of dancing etiquette by leaving a generous gap between them, and looked supremely happy as they glided across the floor. Soon another couple joined them, and then another. Sure enough, Riley Woodboro ambled up to Callie.

"Uh, may I have this dance?" Callie nodded. She didn't have the heart – or nerve – to turn him down. She herself wasn't a good dancer but was pleasantly surprised that through Riley's skillful lead, she began to relax and enjoy her first dance of the night. When the music stopped, Riley thanked her and guided her back to where Sarah Jo was standing.

"Did your shoes survive?" asked Sarah Jo as she looked down at Callie's feet.

"Yes, they did," chuckled Callie. "They're no worse for wear, as my grandmother used to say about stuff."

"You looked like you weren't suffering too much," said Sarah Jo, lowering her voice as a couple girls walked by to get refreshments.

"Naw, it coulda been worse for sure," declared Callie. Both girls danced several times over the course of the evening. The nice thing was, thought Callie, there were no "popular" girls that the guys gravitated to. This type of dance was about having a good time without the pressure of having to be popular or the best looking like some of the dances Callie had heard about that were held at other venues.

At the end of the dance, Beacon Community Church's Pastor Frye went to the microphone and thanked all who had come and had made it an enjoyable occasion. He promised that there would be more dances in the future since this one had been such a success. The time was five minutes to ten, so Callie and Sarah Jo hurried outside to the front of the church. True to her word, Mrs. Foster was waiting for them in the silver SUV. The girls climbed in, still excited about the first dance they'd attended.

CHAPTER TWO

It was midsummer when Callie discovered that Mom and Dad were having problems in their marriage. Naturally, it was very upsetting to Callie who took their family for granted. It would just always be there – Mom and Dad and herself. But these days she'd wake up to the raised voices of her parents and sometimes out and out arguing. Oftentimes there'd be bickering right in front of her which always made her uncomfortable. And about such stupid things!

"Amanda, do I have any clean work socks or aren't you doing the wash lately?"

"They're right in your drawer as usual, Bruce. No need to lay a guilt trip on me." Sometimes they'd start something at dinner, which usually turned to stone cold silence. That was really hard to sit through, thought Callie. I wonder what's wrong with them. One night she heard a conversation between them when they must have thought she was sleeping. Their voices carried from the living room and she could hear them quite well.

"Listen Amanda, I've taken just about all I can take. My workload is heavier than ever since they've downsized at the plant. I have a new supervisor, a Rhonda Blair who thinks that being in charge of men is a real head trip. Plus our latest car repair has set us back. How can a guy get ahead?"

"Well Bruce, all I can say is that you can only do your best – God expects no more, well, except to put your faith in Him to carry you through."

"My best may not be good enough this time," said Dad. "One more thing and it might be the straw that broke the camel's back." That part worried Callie. She'd never thought of Dad being at his breaking point. He was always so strong and steadfast. She'd never heard him talk like this before. Callie turned over and slept fitfully.

By the time Callie got up for breakfast, Dad had already left for work. Mom was busy with laundry.

"Good morning, dear," she said. "You don't look too rested." Callie didn't feel rested either, but she wasn't going to tell Mom why. Just as well to leave things as they were.

"I think I'm going to do something with Sarah Jo today. She didn't call, did she?"

"No Callie," said Mom. "I would've told you if she had."

"Okay, well, I'm going to call her and then eat breakfast. If you want me to help with the clothes I can do that this morning." She kind of felt sorry for Mom, especially in light of the problems she and Dad were having. She'd been laid off from her job, but hoped to be called back soon.

"I'd appreciate that, honey. More hands lighten the load." Yes, Sarah Jo *did* want to get together with Callie and would, in fact, meet her over at Connie's Cocoa Cottage at one o'clock.

*****

Sarah Jo was already there by the time Callie had arrived. She was sitting in a corner booth sipping on a soda.

"Hiya Cal," Sarah Jo greeted her friend brightly.

"Hi," returned Callie less than enthusiastically. "I'm going to get a root beer.

Be right back." She returned and slid in across from Sarah Jo.

"So, how's it going? You look like you lost your best friend," declared Sarah Jo.

"No," said Callie, "you're still with me."

"Why wouldn't I be?"

"I was just kidding, Sarah Jo." She sipped the foam off the top of her root beer. "Have you ever thought about what it would be like if your parents split up?" "Uhh *nooo*," replied Sarah Jo. "Have you? I mean why did you ask me that?" Sarah Jo dabbed her lips with her napkin whether they needed it or not.

"My parents are, well, kinda acting weird," declared Callie.

"*Weird?* What do you men by weird?"

"Like fighting, you know, arguing and stuff."

"Should I be worried about the 'and stuff' part?" asked Sarah Jo.

"You know what I mean," retorted Callie impatiently. "Let's just say they aren't being the nicest to each other, especially Dad."

"What do you mean by not being the nicest to each other? No one can be nice *all* the time," asserted Sarah Jo.

"*Your* parents are," proclaimed Callie.

"How would *you* know? You're not around them all the time."

"I just know is all," said Callie firmly.

"What do your parents argue about?" asked Sarah Jo. "Wait a minute. It's really none of my business."

"Yes it is. You're my friend. Plus you could be praying about it."

"I can still pray about it – and I will, but I don't have to know all the details," said Sarah Jo. A couple of older women came in and sat in the booth next to theirs. Then they went to the counter to order, and returned with hot fudge sundaes.

"You know, I can't figure it out," whispered Callie. "The place is empty except for us and where do these women sit? Practically on top of us!"

"Maybe it's our magnetic personalities," chuckled Sarah Jo.

"Well anyway, what I was saying was that my dad is complaining about how hard he's working when Mom can't help it that she got laid off."

"Does she know when she might be called back?" asked Sarah Jo as she drank the last of her soda.

"Nope," answered Callie. "But wait a minute, I'm not done. There's this chick down at work who bosses him around, a Rhonda Blair."

"Ssshhh…" cautioned Sarah Jo under her breath. "One of those women just looked around at you." That woman approached the booth.

"Excuse me, girls, but did I just hear my name mentioned?" asked the woman whose platinum blonde hair was styled in a chic but tidy hairdo. Callie's jaw dropped noticeably.

"Ummm…. I didn't know it was *your* name," answered Callie.

"Well, let's make this fair. What is *your* name?" The tall slender woman who was fashionably dressed was pleasant enough, thought Callie, so she answered her.

"It's nice to meet you, Callie Morris," said Rhonda Blair as she extended her hand. "Enjoy your day. I'm on a late lunch with my friend here, Linda Simmons. So I must hurry along." Callie wondered if she should introduce Sarah Jo but then thought better of it. No need to take her time if she was in a hurry.

"Wow!" said Sarah Jo after the women had left. "I mean like bigtime wow!"

"No kidding!" replied Callie. "Well, I guess that's a lesson learned."

"How so? You mean mentioning her name?"

"Of course I mean mentioning her name!" hissed Callie.

"Hey, you don't have to take it out on *me*? I didn't do anything wrong."

"Sorry, it's just that – oh, never mind!" snapped Callie. She knew this incident was going to come back to haunt her. She just didn't realize how soon.

CHAPTER THREE

Callie had plenty of time to imagine all kinds of scenarios before her father got home. What if this Rhonda Blair fired him on the spot? Or maybe this Rhonda would just confront her father and leave him to do the damage control from Callie's embarrassing misstep. Her questions were answered soon enough at the dinner table that night.

"This spaghetti is delicious, Mandy. Did you make it differently this time?" asked Dad.

"I guess I did if you count trying another brand of spaghetti sauce," replied Mom.

"Well, I hope you continue to use this recipe – uh brand – from now on," teased Dad. "What do you think, Callie?"

"It's good, Dad, really yummy." The truth was she could hardly taste it, since she was so intent on waiting for the other shoe to fall. She figured this was the calm before the storm. She didn't think she'd get away with having said what she did at Connie's Cocoa Cottage earlier. Callie had acknowledged her wrongdoing before God, but she expected there would be consequences as there almost always is when one does wrong or uses bad judgment.

"Funny thing today, Mandy. Remember what I told you last night about my supervisor? Well, this morning she was all growls, but this afternoon when she came back from lunch she was as nice as you can imagine," said Dad, finishing the last of his spaghetti with gusto.

"Really!" declared Mom. "I wonder what brought the change."

"Well, I'm sure it didn't hurt that I prayed on my way to work. It's just like a transformation took place right before my eyes," said Dad.

Callie couldn't believe what she was hearing. She thought for sure that his supervisor was going to do something awful. Maybe God had something else in mind. She herself knew that she would never again be telling tales about someone she didn't know –especially when she brought it right from a private conversation that didn't involve her. She never heard her father mention Rhonda Blair in a negative way again.

As summer progressed, the time had come to discuss her home school curriculum with Mom. So far, in the last few years, Callie had been able to take charge of her lessons without Mom's supervision, which is why Mom had been able to work. Then, in the evening, after Mom got home, if there were any questions or one-on-one involvement needed Mom was there. Callie's courses required the use of the internet so she was busy with studies during what public school hours required. Mom and Dad had made it clear if she didn't take her schooling seriously, she'd be sent to where she *would* – public school! Callie could barely stand the thought of it after all these years of being taught at home. She wasn't about to mess things up now. She had a few friends in public school and they had asked her why she didn't like going to *their* school. Callie answered that it wasn't so much that she didn't like it, it was just that she was used to home school. But when one of her friends, Donna, persisted, Callie told her what had happened to Sarah Jo and being bullied when she went to school in Addison. Donna insisted that had to be an exaggeration, and that things couldn't have happened that way. But Callie knew Donna's mother was on the school board, which probably influenced Donna's view on the subject.

"So, what do you think, dear? Will this be too much for you to handle?" asked Mom as she searched her daughter's eyes.

"No Mom, this is fine. I can do this, especially if I pace myself. Remember, I can do my work anytime here at home," answered Callie.

"Well, that's true," concurred Mom.

*****

Mom and Dad still argued from time to time, but just not as loudly or as often. So Callie figured things must be improving. Maybe it had something to do with that Rhonda Blair treating Dad better. Then one Monday afternoon Mom got the call she'd been waiting for. She was needed back at work. She was to report in on the following Monday. That seemed to breathe new life into her parents. Once again, things seemed to be back to normal. The Monday Mom was going back to work would be the same day that school began in the district – and for Callie. The phone rang. It was Sarah Jo.

"Hi Cal, how's it going?" asked Sarah Jo.

"Fine, I guess," answered Callie.

"Hey look, I've got an invitation for you. I called Wendy and invited her and Laura to come visit on Thursday. I asked Mom if I could have a sleepover and she said it was okay. Do you want to come?"

"Uh, sure. Let me ask Mom quick just to be sure." Callie set the phone down. In the background Sarah Jo could hear Callie hollering for her mother, then a distant conversation.

"Hey Mom, Sarah Jo's going to have a sleepover and invited Wendy and Laura. Can I go?"

"Sure, Callie, as long as it's okay with Sarah Jo's parents," said Mom.

"It is." Sarah Jo heard Callie pick up the phone. "Mom says it's okay." "I know. I heard you ask her," giggled Sarah Jo.

"Sarah Jo, you're too funny," laughed Callie.

Callie could hardly wait until the sleepover. For one thing, they were fun, and for another, she'd be seeing Wendy and Laura again.

Mrs. Morris dropped Callie off at Sarah Jo's. Callie, with her backpack slung over one shoulder, knocked on the Fosters' side door. Sarah Jo let her in.

"Hey Cal," she said as she eyeballed the backpack, "moving in permanently?" Both girls laughed. "Mom went to pick up Wendy and Laura at the bus station. I said I'd stay here and wait for you. Come to think of it, I guess Mom coulda picked you up too."

"Well, I guess it doesn't matter now," replied Callie. "Hey, what smells so good? You baking something?"

"Yep, some chocolate chip peanut butter cookies. Sound good?"

Sarah Jo took a cookie sheet dotted with the finished product out of the oven.

"Hey, I could eat the cookies, pan and all," said Callie

"You might find it a little hard to digest," chuckled Sarah Jo. "Here, have a cookie. Tell me what you think."

"Mmmm good. Better than the pan for sure."

"Yeh, not too bad – especially when you follow the recipe," added Sarah Jo. "There's Mom. That sure timed out right." At that moment the door opened and Wendy and Laura were there with Mom in tow.

"Go right in, girls. Make yourself comfortable. I see Sarah Jo's cookies are done. Help yourself," said Mom. "Where's Mark?"

"Mark's *here*. I followed my nose down to the source," smiled Sarah Jo's wily brother as he helped himself to a couple of cookies.

"Hey, these are for my sleepover, you little thief," exclaimed Sarah Jo.

"All right, all right," Mark fired back, munching. "I'll make myself scarce." Sarah Jo poured some milk into tumblers and put half the pan of cookies on a plate.

"Come and sit down for a while," said Sarah Jo. "We'll take your stuff to my room later."

"Wow! That's a novel idea – sitting down," mocked Laura. "I've only been doing that for the last three hours."

"No kidding," agreed Wendy, giggling.

"Hey, you two can stand if you want," retorted Sarah Jo. "I've been standing up making these cookies." They all laughed.

"And worth every second," added Callie as she took a sip of milk.

"You should've been on the bus, you guys," said Laura. "There was this drunk. I mean he *smelled* like booze."

"In that case, I'm glad I wasn't," said Sarah Jo.

"I'll second that," said Callie.

"It was hard not to feel sorry for him," said Wendy. "He really looked wasted."

"How come they let him on the bus?" asked Callie.

"Well, for one thing, he was a paying customer. There are people who take buses even if they're sick, so maybe he just looked like he was out of it," said Wendy.

"I sure wouldn't want someone on *my* bus, if they were sick – *or* drunk!" declared Callie. The conversation resumed at dinner, with Sarah Jo's father weighing in on the discussion.

"I don't know that we should judge these people too harshly. After all, we don't know their circumstances," he said. "Could be that they came from a bad background or have fallen on hard times. It doesn't excuse it, but it may explain it to some degree."

"I don't want any drunk to sit by *me* on a bus," declared Mark as he helped himself to more lasagna.

"Nobody does, dear," said Mom. "But can you imagine sitting there reading your Bible next to him?"

"No way!" exclaimed Mark. "Never gonna happen!"

"Yeh," said Sarah Jo. "That's cuz you don't read it – period."

"Sarah Jo," said Mom. "That's not so." Wendy stifled a giggle. This was probably as close to an argument as the Foster family got. After dinner, the girls went for a walk. They reached a nearby park and found some benches. Laura perched on a picnic table.

"So," said Wendy, "what's happening with the Heaven Club here – anything exciting?"

"Sure," answered Sarah Jo. "It's coming along."

"What does that mean?" asked Callie.

"You should know," said Sarah Jo. "You were in on it."

"Things have been going well in Addison," said Wendy. "Quite a few people attend."

"Cool," said Sarah Jo.

"My dad usually goes too. He said it really makes a lot of sense after what happened to him with the tornado. He figures he's just lucky to be alive," continued Wendy.

"I don't know about luck," said Callie. "Maybe more like blessed. He could've ended up like that neighbor you talk about whose place was blown away."

"True," said Wendy.

"Yeh," chimed in Laura. "I saw what was left of his place. Nothing really there."

"That's pretty scary," said Sarah Jo, "to have life go on same-old, same-old one day and the next it's all gone."

"Yeh, who knew that tornado would be coming through right there at that time?" said Laura.

"So, are you guys looking forward to school?" asked Callie of Wendy and Laura. Just then a maple leaf drifted slowly down and settled on Wendy's head. The other three laughed as Wendy plucked it off.

"Sure, I'm just chomping at the bit, as Grandma would say," said Wendy as she contorted her face in mock torment.

"Me too," nodded Laura. "Can hardly wait."

"You guys have it good with your home school," said Wendy.

"Hey, it's work just like public school," said Callie. "Just that we don't have teachers watching over us or go to a building every day."

"Lucky you!" declared Laura.

"We also don't get the chance that you do to let your light shine," explained Callie. "I mean that's pretty important."

"Yeh, but lost on guys like Andy and Damian," asserted Wendy as she picked apart another leaf which had fallen next to her.

"I don't know, Wendy," said Laura. "I think my brother Frankie being in jail got their attention."

"Do you really?" asked Wendy. "I mean those guys are losers with a capital L."

"Well, I guess no one is hopeless as long as they're still drawing breath," commented Sarah Jo. A mosquito had settled on her forearm which she promptly pinged off with her finger.

"You know, Laura, you could make that your project – pray for them, and maybe even talk to them at some point," said Sarah Jo.

"Oh sure, like I could go up to them and just lay it on them. I can hear it now. Hey guys, ever think about salvation?" Laura shook her head. "You must be dreaming, Sarah Jo."

"Well, just remember what *you* can't do, God *can*. You can still be the instrument He uses. Just tell God that you're willing," said Sarah Jo.

"Well, I spose I could do that part," conceded Laura.

"Hey, I've got a great idea," said Callie. The three others were all ears. "Let's get back to the house while we still have enough blood to get there. These mosquitoes are vicious!"

Later, the girls held their own version of a Heaven Club meeting and each had an "assignment" to accomplish to the best of their ability. Laura, of course, would be working on Andy and Damian. Wendy would put her best foot forward not only in school academically and otherwise, but witness by example to Katie Elkins who hired her for occasional babysitting for her daughter Heather. Sarah Jo and Callie said they would work together in helping some elderly people who might need assistance with various chores. Sarah Jo said her Mom volunteered down at the Pine Moor Senior Center a couple days a week and she could find people in need of help around the house or running errands. So, it was all settled. Each one had their mission and they determined that by the time they all met again, they'd each have a progress report. Laura winced, but promised to do her best in spite of the fact that she felt her assignment was the hardest.

The sleepover was, to the girls' way of thinking, a total success – lots of food, lots of talk, and now, plans for each of them to follow through on. Some people might think it was corny, so they kept those plans to themselves. If any of them were having problems with their "missions" they could go to one another for advice or just a different perspective. If they absolutely had to, they could consult with their pastor and get his take on it. Callie hoped it wouldn't come to that, as did Laura. But all resolved to do their very best in carrying out the various tasks ahead.

It was a challenge that would test at least a couple of them.

CHAPTER FOUR

"Okay, are you all set?" asked Mom as she picked up her lunch kit and headed toward the door for work. "If you need anything while I'm at work just text me and I'll call back as soon as I can."

"Sure Mom, whatever," answered Callie casually. There was nothing that was going to require "Mommy's" help, she was confident.

"All right then. Bye dear."

"Bye Mom." Callie gathered the breakfast dishes from the breakfast nook. She guessed Dad liked the omelet she'd made for him as there was not a scrap to be found on his plate. She took the dishes to the sink and began to organize her school day. Algebra would be first because it was the hardest. However, most of it would be review to start with, a carry-over from last year's math. It just so happened that she liked math and its relatives, even plane geometry. She was good at English but Latin posed a challenge. Mom and Dad both wanted her to take the subject since it was available, although not in the local public school. That was too bad since she'd have no one to help her – let alone to complain to – among her friends. It had been a part of Sarah Jo's curriculum but her father felt it was best to wait another year before taking first year Latin. Actually, Callie couldn't see the point in taking it at all and told Sarah Jo that there were no Romans she'd be needing to talk to in that language. They both laughed. Then Sarah Jo said it had to do with it being the foundation of many languages and that a lot of words were derived from Latin roots.

Callie sat down at the computer in the family office. She had a mug of mint tea to keep her company. It was good. She thought she heard a faint knock on the front door. She couldn't imagine who it might be and dismissed it and continued with her studies. This time it was louder, so she went to see who it might be. She peeked behind the curtain on the front window. There was a nicely dressed woman and a little girl – one that was too young for school, but maybe more like daycare age. It might be someone in trouble so she opened the door.

"Good morning," said the tall woman with dull blond hair who was younger than Mom. "My name is Fern Samuels and this is my daughter Olivia." She tugged the little girl's hand and coached her under her breath, "Say hi, honey."

"Hi honey!" blurted out Olivia. Fern Samuels and Callie laughed while Olivia stood looking perplexed.

"I guess you're wondering why I'm here. If you have a moment I'll be glad to tell you," said the plain looking but neatly groomed woman. Olivia fidgeted by her side.

"Well, I am sort of busy right now but if you make it quick – my mother isn't here right now. I'm not allowed to invite strangers in either," said Callie.

"Oh, that's quite all right," replied Fern Samuels. "It's a beautiful day and nice to be out. I just wanted to leave a couple of magazines with you. They're easy to read and certainly timely in this day and age."

"Magazines?" asked Callie. She had enough to read already.

"Yes, share them with your parents when you get done, and neighbors after that if you care to. They're free of charge."

"Mommy – got to go potty," pleaded Olivia tugging her mother's hand.

"Oh dear," said Fern Samuels. "I thought I asked if you had to go before we left home."

"Mommmmmy!" shreiked Olivia.

"Would you mind terribly?" asked Fern Samuels as she edged her way to the open door.

"No, come on in," said Callie. "Down the hall, the first door to your left." What could she do? This was an emergency. A few minutes later, mother and daughter returned, both looking relieved.

"I can't thank you enough. I wasn't expecting that. By the way, what might your name be?"

"Callie."

"Callie," she repeated, "what a nice name."

"Thank you, uh Ms. Samuels," said Callie

"Oh, please call me Mrs. Samuels. I would prefer it." Callie couldn't imagine why that would be necessary. She didn't plan to be seeing her again."

"Oh, here are the magazines I mentioned, Callie. Read them yourself and, as I said, just pass them along. But before you do, jot down my name and number in case you want to call me." This was becoming stranger by the minute to Callie's way of thinking. What was the point in all this? Finally she and Olivia left, leaving Callie to wonder if she shouldn't be so quick to answer the door next time.

She set the magazines down on the table next to the door. It was usually where the day's mail ended up. One of the titles of the articles caught her eye – *Are Our Young People Going to the Dogs?* What a strange title for an article in a magazine. She opened the magazine to the page where the article could be found. An image of a couple of teenagers romping with a collie and a golden retriever greeted her eyes. Underneath the picture it said: *Allison and Grant exercise shelter dogs.* What was the name of the magazine? In bold bright letters it said *AWARE!* Callie had never heard of that one before, but it seemed interesting. Maybe she'd read the article later but for now she had to get back to her studies.

The rest of the day was uneventful, which was fine with Callie. She had at least gotten her algebra assignment finished. She wondered how Sarah Jo's day had gone. Maybe she'd just send a quick email to find out. She might even tell her about her visitors earlier.

"Hello dear," announced Mom as she entered the back door. "How was your day, run into any snags?"

"Snags?" repeated Callie.

"Well, you know, problems of some sort with your first day."

"Not really," said Callie. "Most everything is a review at this point."

"Oh, I suppose so. Well, I'm glad we both had a good first day. Come and help me fix dinner, would you, dear?

The front door swung open and heralded the arrival of Dad. Callie wondered if he would see the magazines on the table next to the door.

"Hey, what's this?" asked Dad. "*AWARE!* Probably just more junk mail." Callie saw from the kitchen that he threw that and the other magazine into the leather-look wastebasket on the other side of the table. "So, how are my girls today on this first day of school *and* work?

"Doing well," answered Mom. "Callie here seemed to have a good day. Mine wasn't too bad either."

"Great! I suppose we should celebrate," said Dad.

"Well, I've already started dinner, but we can have a good time eating it," laughed Mom.

"What's on the menu?"

"Chicken cacciatore, Dad," replied Callie.

"Mmmm.... one of my favorites!" Later at dinner, Dad brought up the magazines.

"Wonder where those magazines came from - no return address and, in fact, no mailing address. Callie, do you know anything about them?"

"Kinda," she said. She explained about the woman at the door and her little girl.

"So you let them in?" asked Mom.

"I had to. The girl had to go to the bathroom."

"Well, you did the right thing. You really had no choice. Who were they?"

"I have no idea, Mom. She told me her name. I know the little girl's name was Olivia." She nibbled on her chicken.

"See, here's the thing, Callie," began Dad. "Something like that – although not likely in this little town - could be a set-up. There are people who stay awake nights trying to figure out various crimes."

"What do you mean, Dad?"

"Well, let me give you an example. Years ago I knew a family in our neighborhood where the mother stayed at home. One day a door-to-door salesman came by the house. This mother let him in. He had a product case and was very convincing in his sales pitch, but what he was really doing was casing the joint, as they say. He wanted to know what kind of valuables were in the home. The thing is, he was actually peddling some cheap silver polish. When he asked to demo his product he was able to find out that she had sterling silverware as well as a few pieces of nice jewelry. Next thing we knew, he had burglarized their home when they were at church the next Sunday."

"Did they ever catch him?" asked Callie.

"No, I don't think they did. Back in those days communications were not as advanced as now. The authorities have far more tools in terms of technology at their disposal than they did back then."

"So what does that have to do with me, Dad?"

"Well, believe it or not, Callie, in the real world women can be criminals too. Or they can help their man by being an accomplice. Some of them are really hardened too. Their consciences are seared. The woman could be doing the same thing as that salesman. Or worse, the man could appear on the scene and kidnap you."

"Oh Bruce, you'll frighten her. That is not a likely scenario," declared Mom.

"Not likely, Amanda, but if something *did* happen to her we'd regret it for the rest of our lives that we hadn't been more emphatic about teaching her not to allow strangers in our home."

"Well, you do make a good point, I have to admit," said Mom. "From here on in, *no one* and I do mean *no one* is allowed in unless we're here. And if a stranger comes to the door when we're here we'll handle it, do you understand?"

"Yes Mom," said a cowed-down Callie. She wished she'd thrown those stupid magazines into the wastebasket to begin with.

CHAPTER FIVE

Callie set her pride aside and told Sarah Jo about the magazine incident. She wondered what Sarah Jo would've done if she was in *her* shoes.

"Gosh, I don't know," said Sarah Jo slowly. "We have the same rule over here – no strangers in the house when my parents are gone. I don't know what I would've done."

"Well, I could hardly turn them away under the circumstances," declared Callie as she gripped her cell phone tighter. "I mean the little girl really had to go."

"I wouldn't sweat it," consoled Sarah Jo. "By the way, who *were* those people?"

"I'm not sure. Prob'ly from some church. Their magazines were sort of religious looking," replied Callie.

"Did you tell them you have a church you go to?"

"I didn't have time to think. I was starting my algebra when I heard a knock at the door. I didn't know if it was a package being delivered or what," explained Callie. "I'd have just been better off ignoring it."

"True, but if your parents were expecting something they might've been ticked if you hadn't answered the door. Some days you just can't win, right?"

"You got that right, Sarah Jo. Hey, have you heard from Wendy or Laura?"

"Laura sent me an email. She said Andy and Damian are hopeless as far as witnessing to them," chuckled Sarah Jo. "I know she's just kidding but I'm glad I don't have to do that."

"No kidding!" agreed Callie.

"As for Wendy, Laura says that Mrs. Elkins has really been nice to her since she agreed to come back and baby sit for her daughter. I think her name is Heather."

"Well, at least there's good news on that front. This really is like a battle. Makes you wonder why people are so resistant to God; I mean considering all He has done for them."

"Ignorance, my dear Callie – that and human nature. The Bible tells us that it's at odds with God," said Sarah Jo.

"Well, I suppose I'd better get back to the books. This year I want to keep up, if not get ahead, if I can," said Callie.

"I know what you mean," replied Sarah Jo.

"Hey, I've got a question. I mean it's great that we don't have the distractions like we would in regular school, but do you ever miss having guys around?"

"Whoooaa, where's that coming from? Did you see the guy of your dreams?"

"Sarah Jo! I was just asking is all," said Callie. There was silence for a moment.

"Of course I think about guys, but I look at it this way. Having a boyfriend is not the best thing ever – you are! Well, God is, but I'm just saying that this is a time to put yourself first as far as your future is concerned. Do you remember Debbie Miller from church? She had a boyfriend. She-"

"Yeh, I know who she is," interrupted Callie.

"Well, she told me at Sunday School that he turned out to be a jerk. I mean he was bossing her around and spying on her, that kind of stuff," said Sarah Jo.

"I bet he wasn't a believer," said Callie.

"I don't think so, but that's all the more reason to hold out for someone who's decent and has values. I'm perfectly content to go to dances that have been set up by our church – stuff like that."

"I guess you're right," conceded Callie. "I wouldn't want to go through what Debbie did."

*****

Later that afternoon Mom asked Callie if she could run an errand for her. They would be having spaghetti for dinner and Mom needed some mushrooms and also a loaf of Italian bread. Could she run to the store and get the items for her?

"Sure Mom. You want fresh or canned mushrooms?"

"I'd prefer fresh, dear."

"Okay, I'll take my bike and go to Phil's Supermarket. Be back in a flash," said Callie. It didn't take long to get to the store that was less than a mile away.

She parked her bike and locked it to a nearby tree.

"Well hello, young lady." It was Fern Samuels. "Olivia, say hello to our new friend here."

Friend? thought Callie. Fern Samuels' request went unheeded. Instead Olivia had found the brightly colored boxes of cereals across from the canned goods to be far more interesting. "By the way, did you get a chance to read the magazines I left with you?"

"Uh, not yet," replied Callie. She'd not read through any of the contents of either magazine.

"Mommy, can we buy these?" Olivia deposited a multi-colored box of cereal in her mother's cart.

"No dear," said Fern Samuels. "We don't eat that kind of junk."

"Well, I think I'd better get going," said Callie. "Mom needs some things for dinner."

"Oh, then you must be going," said Mrs. Samuels, as she followed Callie. "If I can be so bold, may I suggest that next time you shop for bread, that you skip this white stuff. It just clogs you up."

"Really?" asked Callie incredulously. She inspected the loaf.

"Oh yes, dear. And read the label. These bakers slip in animal fat, like lard. You know, we really shouldn't eat things like that."

"Uh, I didn't know that. We only buy this when we have spaghetti or Italian stuff," said Callie.

"Oh my, you'd be surprised what sits on these shelves. Just read the labels sometime. And as for the meat department, well, I won't even go into that."

"I've got to go now. Bye," said Callie as she turned to go to the checkout.

"Goodbye. I hope we see each other again," said Mrs. Samuels. "Now Olivia, put those boxes of cereal back right now!"

Callie decided she wouldn't tell Mom or Dad about her encounter with Fern Samuels and her daughter at the supermarket. Why stir things up? It could all have been avoided had she not answered the door to begin with that first day of home school. It would sure be nice to know the consequences of doing things in advance. Once outside the store, she slipped the mushrooms and bread into her backpack and went on her way. She hoped she wouldn't run into that woman and her daughter again; she felt uncomfortable around them.

Dinner was good, if uneventful. Callie listened as her parents got into a spiritual discussion of sorts. It had to do with a lady in the church who'd confided in Mom, but she didn't say who it was.

"I just don't think she was being honest, Mandy – plain and simple," said Dad. "A woman who buys things and hides them – except for Christmas or birthday presents – is being very sneaky and under-handed."

"I guess she just figures it's part of her pay for all she does at home, like taking care of the kids, laundry, fixing meals – that kind of thing."

"She probably does deserve something, but unless the guy's a mil-lionaire this is really going to compromise their budget."

"I see your point, Bruce, but she said if she told her husband about this, he'd really go through the roof." Mom passed the fragrant garlic bread around for takers.

"That's the whole point, though. The reason he'd go ballistic is be-cause he knows the budget can't handle it. Plus, he'd feel she was doing something behind his back, which she is. After all, if you compromise your integrity you are no longer who you say you are."

"That's true," agreed Mom.

"I know I can always trust you, Mandy. We're in this together. Marriage is for adults, not kids playing hide and seek."

"I feel uncomfortable about her telling me this. I mean it may make *her* feel better but I feel like I know a secret I shouldn't be keeping," said Mom.

"Well, she's put you in an awkward position for sure, by telling you. I almost want to say that you should identify who this is so that I can tell her husband. But I don't think butting in at this point would serve any real purpose except to stir up a hornet's nest and I don't want that. But Mandy, you're in a unique position to steer her in the right direction, especially if she comes to you again."

"I don't know if she'd take my advice, Bruce. But I suppose I could try."

"Well, I'd be subtle about it; no need to shoot off like a cannon which I know you wouldn't. But make it clear enough that she gets the point. In the meantime, we'll keep her and her husband in our prayers. This could turn out to be a major breach in their marriage if it goes on for too long."

"Dad, couldn't you and Mom go to Pastor Martin and explain what's going on with a 'hypothetical' couple?"

"I was just about to mention that, Callie. If nothing else works, I think that would be the next step. Mandy, do you know if she told anyone else what she told you or was another woman with you when she told you these things?"

"No, it was just me."

"Well, we'll all keep that couple in our prayers and see what happens. God can do miracles, even in a situation like this," said Dad.

*****

Callie called Sarah Jo after she'd loaded the dinner dishes into the dishwasher. She decided to get her take on the situation. It's not that it bothered her so much as it begged an answer. It was like the Bible principle of there being wisdom with a multitude of counselors. Since it wasn't her own responsibility to fix what was wrong, Callie felt no pressure in kicking the subject around. She explained the dinner discussion to Sarah Jo.

"And you're telling me this *why* exactly?"

"No real reason. Just wondering what you think of it is all," said Callie.

"Well, I'll tell you one thing- it sure isn't *my* parents. Mom would never do that to my father."

"No, I know that would never happen in your family," agreed Callie.

"Okay, to answer your question, I think that's kind of sneaky to do that kind of thing. I mean if you do it once, that's bad enough, but to do it regularly that's what my dad would call an attitude problem. It'll catch up to her sooner or later for sure," predicted Sarah Jo.

CHAPTER SIX

Callie found that home school this year was easier than what she thought it would be. Algebra was challenging at times, but nothing she couldn't overcome when she applied herself. She was glad she didn't stand in the way of Mom's job, and that she could pretty much do her schooling on her own. Most of it was done by computer so she always had resources available for help when she needed it. One day in late September Callie went out to rake leaves while it was daylight. It wasn't a particularly cold day and the sun warmed her. She thought amusedly that this worked nicely for Phy Ed and she certainly got a workout with such a big yard. She took a moment to rest and watched a squirrel on the other side of the yard feverishly burying an acorn under the leaves. She hoped the squirrel buried it in the dirt since she didn't want to rake up his winter food supply.

"Well hello," came a familiar voice from over the split rail fence. It was Fern Samuels! "I was just out enjoying our beautiful weather; perfect weather for a walk." "Hi," said Callie feebly. She noted that the little girl wasn't with her this time.

"So, getting your yard raked up before winter, I see. That's a lot of work for one person," observed Mrs. Samuels.

"I don't mind," replied Callie almost too quickly. She raked a few straggler leaves into the large pile.

"They're hard to get into the bag though. It's a two-man, or woman, job."

"Dad will help me when he comes home." She wished Fern Samuels would just go away and leave her to her raking. But she didn't. Instead she went around the fence to the front of the house and approached Callie; then picked up a leaf bag that was on the ground.

"Here, let me help you with that," said Mrs. Samuels. She held the bag wide open so that Callie could deposit the leaves into it.

"Uh thanks," said Callie as she filled the bag up with leaves. "I'll do the rest later."

"Really? I've got nothing but time on my hands this afternoon. I'd be more than glad to help. For me, it's a way to show my appreciation to the Lord for what He did for me – to help others, that is." Callie began to feel uncomfortable.

"I've really got to get in. I've got things to do before Mom gets home," stammered Callie.

"I've noticed you're not in school, public school that is. Are you taking courses at home?"

"Yes, I'm in home school," said Callie. She guessed it wouldn't be so easy getting away from Mrs. Samuels.

"*Really*? How interesting! Do you like it?"

"Yeh, it's okay. Sometimes I kind of miss being around other kids, but they're not all nice, and I don't miss the bad ones."

"I've thought about that with Olivia. I don't want her mixing in with kids who are going to bring her down. She's young yet, so I don't worry so much, but in the higher grades where there's drugs and bad influences, well, that's different."

"Well, you have plenty of time to make that decision since she's young yet," said Callie.

"True, but I want to get her used to the idea. Not only that, but I don't know that much about it myself," said Mrs. Samuels. "I'd sure appreciate it if you could kind of clue me in. If I prepare now, I'll be ready to deal with Olivia when the time comes."

"Right. Well, I suppose I could tell you how it's worked for me and my family, but things keep changing."

"I realize that, Callie, but I also know that some of the basic principles don't change, and that's what I need help with."

"You could always search home schooling on your computer," suggested Callie.

"Oh, we don't have a computer, dear. Just not into that new-fangled stuff".

"Well, I suppose you could go to the library for that, but you'd just about have to get one if Olivia is in home school," added Callie.

"I guess I'll cross that bridge when I come to it," replied Mrs. Samuels. "Say, before I go, I wonder if I could ask a favor of you – or at least consider it."

"Uh, I don't know. I'm pretty busy with school and all. "Callie scrambled to find the words to get out of whatever Mrs. Samuels was wanting. She didn't want to be any more involved than she was.

"Of course you are, dear," responded Mrs. Samuels sympathetically. "I have no right to ask anything of you. I just thought if you had a Saturday afternoon free that maybe you could come and talk to our young people about your home school experience."

"Well uh, maybe sometime," said Callie, hoping to put off Mrs. Samuels.

"Sure, that would be fine. Maybe sometime next month?"

"I don't know. I guess you could check back." Now why did she have to go and say *that?*

"What's your phone number, dear?" she asked, poised with a pen and scrap of paper. Callie, not knowing how to get out of it, rattled off her cell phone number.

"I'll be in touch," said Mrs. Samuels, waving. Great, thought Callie. She got me again! Well, an hour or so talking to kids about home school wouldn't hurt anything. In fact, it might be good experience to connect with the community, not to mention hone her public speaking skills, even if it was just a small group.

*****

"Sarah Jo," whined Callie later on the phone, "I walked right into it. Now she's got my number."

"So, what's the problem with that? You want her to contact you by carrier pigeon?" Both girls giggled.

"No," said Callie. "I just don't want her contacting me at all."

"Why not?" asked Sarah Jo. "She doesn't seem to be an evil monster."

"There's just something about her. Hey, I've got it!" exclaimed Callie. "Why don't you come with me to that thing she's putting on about home school?" For a moment there was silence.

"Well, I don't know," hesitated Sarah Jo. "I mean you know her and all. She doesn't know me at all."

"I'll just tell her I have a friend who is in home school too. Pleeeease..." begged Callie.

"Oh okay," caved Sarah Jo. "When is this?"

"I don't know yet; maybe next month."

"Let me know when you know for sure. And don't forget," said Sarah Jo, "next month we'll be having a Heaven Club meeting on Saturday. Pastor Martin will announce it this Sunday."

"Oh yeh, that's right," said Callie.

It was announced at church that the Heaven Club meeting would be the second Saturday in November. Well, that was okay, now Callie knew. If there was a conflict with it and helping Mrs. Samuels, this might be her out. She didn't want to miss even one meeting of the Heaven Club.

At home, the Morris family agreed that the sermon had been one of Pastor's best: the reward of the saved.

"It sounds like something that would tie in with the Heaven Club," said Mom.

"I was thinking the same thing," declared Dad. "That man sure has a way with words. I have to wonder if he isn't researching into the subject more, based on what he said." He helped himself to more chicken wings.

"I wouldn't be at all surprised," said Mom. "Callie, you're sure quiet. What do you think?"

"Uh, I thought the sermon was really good, Mom – not boring at all." Both Mom and Dad gave her an odd look.

"Sermons aren't supposed to be boring, Callie," said Dad. The topic wasn't open for discussion.

"Well, you know what I mean," said Callie.

CHAPTER SEVEN

Callie was excited! The United Home School Group of Pine Moor was going to have a recreation day, a portion of which would be using the public school gym. It was to be held on a Saturday, the one after the Heaven Club meeting would be held. It was close to Thanksgiving but with time enough to squeeze it in. Callie loved gym days at the school. It wasn't that it was her only Phy Ed class. She worked out to a couple of videos every other day during the week. If she and Sarah Jo could find some public school friends who wanted to make a couple of teams, they would do outdoor sports on nice days. Usually though, they would be busy on Saturdays, and now she would be too. So gym day at the school would be a great time to get together with others in home school and enjoy it as a social event as well as for getting exercise.

Callie had just begun reading her American History assignment when her cell phone rang. Of course she had the option to ignore it, but when she noticed it was Fern Samuels she knew she'd get another call interrupting her at some point again. So she answered it.

"Hello."

"Why hello, dear. How are you today?" asked Mrs. Samuels.

"I'm fine, thanks," answered Callie.

"Well, I'm just calling, as I said I would the day you were raking leaves."

"Right," answered Callie. How could she forget? It was only last week.

"I just wanted to let you know I hadn't forgotten, and to let you know when we'll be getting the children together."

"Mrs. Samuels," said Callie. "I'll be busy for the next two Saturdays."

"Really, dear? Did you prioritize?"

"Of course," replied Callie, now getting annoyed at her caller. "My church and school come first on my schedule."

"I'm sure your church would understand that it's a godly thing to reach out to the community, wouldn't it?" pressed Mrs. Samuels.

"S-sure," stammered Callie, "but I have other things going on as well.

"Such as... if I may ask?"

"The Heaven Club," answered Callie all too quickly. She felt like she was on trial and having to defend her decisions.

"The Heaven Club? How interesting! Tell me about it," urged Mrs. Samuels.

"I can't right now," said an irritated Callie. "I have to get back to my school work."

"Well, that's fine, dear," said Mrs. Samuels. "You go on back to what you were doing. I suppose we could hold our gathering the Saturday after Thanksgiving. I'll check with the parents on that."

"That's Thanksgiving weekend though. Don't count on me for that Saturday. Our family might be busy," said Callie.

"Well, we'll see what the good Lord wants," said Mrs. Samuels. "If it's to be then, He will work it out. Goodbye dear." Click.

That call started the day off all wrong. Things didn't get any better by noon. Callie found it hard to concentrate and decided to exercise to a video. That didn't help either. So she sat in the big rocker recliner that Dad usually occupied and found herself praying. She was interrupted by another phone call. Caller ID showed that it was Mom.

"Hi Callie," she said. "I just wanted to ask how things are going."

"Okay, I guess – for a Monday morning."

"Good. I have slow days too," chuckled Mom. "Would you mind taking the chicken casserole out of the freezer for dinner? I'll warm it up when I get home."

"Sure Mom, not a problem."

"Thanks, dear," replied Mom. "See you later." Callie didn't mind at all when Mom called, but Mrs. Samuels, well, this was getting to be a problem. First of all, she should realize that she was calling her during school hours; plus Mrs. Samuels loved to talk. She decided she simply wouldn't take any more of her calls if they were during the day when she was studying. She'd been taught by her parents to show respect for adults; after all, the Bible taught that. But she also needed to fulfill her school requirements if she wanted to continue with home school.

*****

The week went quickly and then came Saturday – the Heaven Club! It was always fun and thought provoking. She and Sarah Jo usually sat together in Fellowship Hall. This Saturday there were quite a few people, mostly teens. It looked as though some kids from Beacon Community Church were in attendance as Pastor Martin said there might be. An invitation had been extended to the youth of that church a couple of weeks prior to the meeting of the Heaven Club. Apparently there was interest.

"Wow Callie," exclaimed Sarah Jo. "Good turnout."

"Yeh, can you believe this all started cuz of us girls?" The pair found a couple chairs near the front and sat down.

"Hard to believe, Cal, but I guess God can do anything- even with people who aren't even looking for something to do spiritually."

"Well, I don't mind doing things for God," said Callie. "I mean that's fine and all, but I want to do other things too."

"I'm sure He knows that," said Sarah Jo. "But the Heaven Club is something, now that it's started, will be of service to others for a long time to come – way beyond whatever you'll be doing in life."

"True," agreed Callie. "I just wonder what I'll be doing then." Pastor Martin approached the front of the room.

"That's what makes life fun, Cal – having God surprise you with all kinds of opportunities and people."

"Good afternoon, young people," greeted Pastor Martin. "What a beautiful day we have out there – and in here – for our Heaven Club meeting. I trust all of you are prepared for some uplifting - no pun intended - information about heaven. We all need to keep focused on the goal."

The meeting, as usual, was great. Afterward, snacks were served and small groups of teens gathered to discuss what they'd heard at the meeting.

Callie noticed that Riley Woodboro had come to the meeting. He seemed to have grown tall or thinner, one or the other. He looked her way briefly and then made his way over to where she and Sarah Jo were standing.

"Hi Callie," his voice boomed. "How's it going?"

"Good. Is this your first Heaven Club meeting?"

"Yep, first one. Hi, Sarah Jo."

"Hi Riley. So, what did you think of it?" asked Sarah Jo.

"I dunno," replied Riley. "Makes sense, I guess. Never much thought about it before."

"Are you glad you came to the meeting?" asked Callie. While he thought about his answer she scanned the room to see if Donnie Maxwell had shown up, but she didn't see him.

"I guess. Like I said, I've never given much thought to this before." "You think you'll come to the next meeting?" asked Sarah Jo.

"Maybe. Depends on what else is going on," answered Riley. "See you around." He ambled off in the direction of the refreshment table.

"Wow, how much fun was *that?*" asked Callie. They both giggled.

"Not much, but it probably took courage to come up and talk to us – well, mainly you."

"Me? No, it was both of us," insisted Callie.

*****

Callie was thoroughly questioned by her parents at dinner about the meeting. The Heaven Club was quite the addition to the church's list of activities – and a popular one.

"Why don't you check it out for yourselves?" asked Callie, really sort of hoping they wouldn't take her up on it.

"Well dear, it's mostly for teens," said Mom.

"Some of the kids' parents come though," said Callie.

"Well, maybe sometime your father and I can make it." It was left at that. No need for someone to go to something unless they really want to or feel they can spare the time.

Life settled into a predictable routine in spite of the approaching holidays. Callie was glad for that, as well as looking forward to the holidays since her school breaks followed those of public school.

Just before Thanksgiving she received a call from Mrs. Samuels who practically begged her to come to the meeting of children and their parents to speak about her experience with home school. Mrs. Samuels didn't want to delay by getting too far into the school year before holding it.

"I just don't know, Mrs. Samuels, our family might have plans as I mentioned before. I'd have to check with Mom and Dad."

"Well, we have things lined up for next Saturday. Everyone will be expecting you," insisted Mrs. Samuels.

"I don't understand why. I never said for sure I could do it."

"Well, I just had faith about it," replied Mrs. Samuels. "Please say you'll come. It starts with a meal at noon. You'll speak at one."

"Well okay, I will if we don't have any plans," said Callie who was now confused with this wrench in the works she'd almost forgotten about. "Where is it being held?"

"It'll be at 1240 Maple Street. It's actually within walking distance of where you live."

"I don't know exactly what to prepare," said Callie who saw this as a disaster in the making.

"It's okay," reassured the older woman. "You have all the preparation you need right inside your brain. We just want to 'pick that brain', as they say."

"Well okay. Good bye," ended Callie abruptly. Well, this was just great. What had she gotten herself into? Of and by itself, it would've been okay. It wasn't okay to have it fall on the Saturday after Thanksgiving. But now she was committed and had to follow through. She'd mention it to Mom and Dad but if she had any notion of pulling out, they wouldn't stand for it. They believed that giving your word and following through was a matter of honor.

*****

Thanksgiving was no small event at the Morris household. It was like the first time since the end of summer and the beginning of the school year that signified a real break. Plus it was one day where the family could all be together on a weekday. That was not a big thing of and by itself, just that it was different and a nice change. Mom went all out on the dinner and Callie was right by her side. The fact that she'd helped seemed to make the meal even more yummy. This year there would be no relatives visiting; most were too far away. A couple years earlier Mom's brother Ted and his wife June came for Thanksgiving. Callie liked Uncle Ted; he was funny. Aunt June was nice too. They always brought a gift from their home state of Florida.

That year it was seashells.

"Of course what we could really use is some nice Florida sunshine for the winter months here," Dad joked.

"Well Bruce, any time you want to transplant the family to Florida, I'll help you any way I can," Uncle Ted had said.

"I'll second that," added Aunt June. Callie knew that would never happen. They had visited there once, but it was a long time ago. It happened to be in summer when Dad had his vacation. All Callie could remember was Dad talking about how hot and humid it was. The only time they were comfortable was inside the air-conditioned house or car.

*****

"Honey, is the gravy thickened up yet?" asked Mom from where she was putting the finishing touches on the yams.

"I think so," said Callie as she lifted the spoon and let the rich gravy run off and back into the pan. "Look."

"Yes, that's fine. You can turn the heat off under it now." Soon they were gathered around the Thanksgiving table, each telling what they were thankful for.

It was kind of corny to Callie's way of thinking but it *did* bring significance to the day. She had to admit there was much to be thankful for. Of course, she was glad she knew God and what Jesus had done for her. Part of the reason she appreciated it was because of the Heaven Club. If heaven was absent from her future, then what did this life count for? She was learning things about heaven that she usually didn't think about. She was also glad for home school. Karen Hopkins who went to public school said that a lot of the kids complained about their parents or that they didn't get to do what they wanted and that sort of thing. She didn't tell Mom and Dad this at the table, but she knew in her heart of hearts she had it good.

"Mmmm..." said Dad. "You two gals have outdone yourselves this year. I'm almost glad we *don't* have company – more leftovers!"

"Well, I think the turkey turned out really well," added Mom. "I cooked it a little differently this year. I'll have to fix it this way every year."

"*What?*" exclaimed Dad sounding mock flabbergasted. "No deep fried turkey?"

"Now Bruce," said Mom, "we'll have one on the Fourth of July when it will shoot up into the sky like a rocket."

"Mom and Dad, what are you talking about?" asked Callie. She knew they were joking but didn't see the point in it.

"Actually dear, it isn't funny at all. If people aren't careful when they deep fry a turkey it can cause a fire," said Mom.

"Yes," said Dad. "People have lost their homes that way."

"Actually," said Mom, "the only advantage I see by doing a turkey that way is the outside of the bird. It's the part that is deep fried. The inside would be cooked just as any other method of cooking."

"Well, promise me that we won't risk life and limb to cook a turkey that way," chuckled Dad. "I like yours just fine."

CHAPTER EIGHT

Callie was not looking forward to this gathering of young people she would be addressing. She had told Sarah Jo when this meeting would be but Sarah Jo's family would be out of town for the whole Thanksgiving weekend. *She* should be so lucky. Oh well, she chided herself, quit complaining. Maybe God would bring something good out of this.

Since it wasn't raining or snowing, only cold, Callie decided to walk to the address Mrs. Samuels had provided. She approached a nondescript building with its most significant features being that it was built of bricks and not very big. There was no sign identifying it as a church. She could hear noise emanating from within and wasn't sure if she should knock or not. So she simply entered, since she was expected anyway. A rush of warm food-fragrant air greeted her and people were crammed in at several tables. One table held pans and crockery pots of hot food.

"Well hello, Callie," greeted Mrs. Samuels. "I'm so glad you're here. I've saved a place for you at my table. Just hang up your coat on the hook over there and serve yourself." Callie wished she could dash out the door and not look back. She could think of a thousand reasons not to be here. Well, maybe not a thousand but enough to get out of it. She hadn't told Mom or Dad where she was going; she figured she didn't need to. She just said she'd be back in a while. They trusted her judgment, especially at her age.

Callie looked at the assortment of food: fluffy mashed potatoes, a noodle casserole of some sort, macaroni and cheese, deviled eggs, green beans and a vegetable plate with dip. One thing was noticeably absent. There didn't seem to be any type of meat. That was okay with her. She'd eaten enough turkey to hold her till next Thanksgiving. It just seemed funny, that's all. A couple of days ago people ate their Thanksgiving turkey. She thought someone might have used some of the leftover turkey in a casserole or something. She took some of the mashed potatoes, an egg and some macaroni and cheese and went to Mrs. Samuels' table; the one with the only vacant seat in the room.

"Did you find enough to eat?" asked Mrs. Samuels. "That's not very much. We have plenty."

"No, this is fine, thanks," answered Callie.

"Well, if you want more when you're done, just go help yourself, dear." Callie had to admit the food was good, even though she wasn't very hungry. She didn't come here to eat. In fact, she wouldn't have eaten anything if it hadn't been for the fact that she might've offended Mrs. Samuels. At 12:45 Mrs. Samuels stood up and announced a last call for food. In a few minutes they would be taking down tables and setting up chairs so everyone needed to be done eating. Callie got up but didn't know if she was to help with setting things up for her to speak, so she took her paper plate and plasticware to the garbage can and deposited them there. Mrs. Samuels told her she could wait at the perimeter of the room until the older boys had taken down the tables and set up the chairs.

At that point Callie was feeling more comfortable among this room of virtual strangers, well, except for Mrs. Samuels. She wasn't really prepared though, and she had no idea what she would tell these young people and the parents who'd accompanied them. Soon the dining room had been transformed into an assembly hall with all the folding chairs lined up neatly in rows.

"Everyone take their seats please," rose Mrs. Samuels' voice above the buzz. "Our special guest speaker is ready to share her adventures in home schooling with all of you. I'd like to present Miss Callie Morris." There was a short applause. Callie took her place at a no-frills podium, one that perhaps one of the men had made at his home workshop. She wished she'd brought some printed material to set before her, but this was going to have to be impromptu since she had nothing prepared for the occasion.

"Hi everyone," said Callie as she looked around the room. "Mrs. Samuels asked me to come speak to you about my experience with home school. I've been in home school since I was six years old. My mom stayed home with me for most of my school career and just recently went back to work. Unlike years ago, home school can mostly be done online, plus it is looked upon more favorably than years ago when you had to get permission form the state DPI... er, the Department of Public Instruction and be able to show a curriculum and schedule." Callie continued providing information, but she noticed a lanky young man sitting in the front. He seemed to hang on every word she said. It was sort of a distraction. The rest of the kids looked interested but not intent like this boy did.

"Now all of you have different situations so that will affect how you view home school as an option. For example, this is the only type of education I really know, so it works well for me. I have a friend, though, who is a Christian believer and she sees it as an advantage to be in public school where she can witness, I guess you'd say, just by example to others. If you have any questions I'll try and answer them for you."

"Thank you, Callie," said Mrs. Samuels. "Our young people generally don't speak until spoken to, but they can consider your invitation to ask questions as permission." A boy in the back raised his hand high above the shock of red hair that seemed to have a mind of its own.

"Yes, uh, how many hours a day do you do home school?"

"It's about the same as public school," answered Callie. "The nice thing is, I can do my work whenever I want to, although I usually follow public school hours." A petite girl with long dark hair raised her hand. Callie nodded in her direction.

"Do you ever go out shopping or anything during regular school hours?"

"Well, I guess I could but I usually don't. Public school kids are in school then, so there's no need to make people wonder if I'm skipping school. I suppose if I *had* to go out, that would be a different story." Then the boy who'd been studying her from the front row raised his hand and began speaking simultaneously.

"So, what are the pros and cons of home school?" he asked

"Good question, Austin," interjected Mrs. Samuels. Callie had to think for a moment. She couldn't think of any downside to home school. Oh well, she'd let her mind get imaginative.

"I suppose you could say the lack of social interaction, but that's not entirely true," declared Callie. "Years ago that was one of the major objections to home school. Home school students still get to do things with friends from public school. Plus we also have organized home school events and activities that bring us in contact with other students that are home schooled."

"What about the pros of homeschooling?" asked Mrs. Samuels.

"Well, I can only speak for myself but I find it's easier to concentrate at home. I also am in charge of making sure I get my assignments done," explained Callie. "If I drop the ball on something this important, my parents will send me to public school to make sure I graduate." A girl in a gray shapeless dress raised her hand.

"Go ahead, Penny," said Mrs. Samuels. Penny fidgeted as if she wasn't sure she wanted to talk or not but finally did.

"Can you go to college if you are home schooled?" she whispered, barely audible.

"I'm sorry," said Callie, "but I didn't hear you." Mrs. Samuels, looking slightly annoyed, repeated the question.

"Oh yes," answered Callie quickly. "I sure *do* plan to go. I just have to have all my credits, plus I'll be getting some guidance counseling on colleges, courses and all that."

"Well," said Mrs. Samuels as she stood up. "This has been very informative. I, on behalf of our youth, would like to thank you for your time in sharing here today, Callie. Okay, young people, don't go just yet. There are some things I'd like to talk about before you leave." Mrs. Samuels escorted Callie to the door and thanked her again. The cold wind slapped her in the face with the realization that winter was just around the corner. All things considered, Callie felt things went reasonably well, at least for her part. For being unprepared, she felt she could've done much worse but, after all, home school was a subject she knew well.

*****

"Where have *you* been?" greeted Dad as Callie walked in the door. She took off her sensible corduroy jacket and matching navy gloves.

"It was just this meeting thing I was invited to," replied Callie.

"Not the Heaven Club; that met just recently, if I recall."

"Dad, it wasn't the Heaven Club. It was something else – a bunch of school age kids wanting to know about home school, so I told them."

"Who was in charge of these kids?" asked Dad. He seemed to be determined to get to the bottom of this.

"Remember that Mrs. Samuels – the one whose little girl needed to use our bathroom that time? Well, it was her church group – the kids, that is."

"What church is that?" asked Dad, shifting in his chair as if it would help him hear his daughter better.

"I don't know the exact name; something like Future Life Fellowship."

"Never heard of it," said Dad with a note of skepticism in his voice. "So, did it go okay?"

"I guess so. I just shared what I know about home school." Callie wanted to escape to her room. She'd had enough questions for one day.

Unfortunately for Callie, the subject came up again at dinner so that she basically had to explain the whole thing all over again to Mom, with a few prompts from Dad. Mom listened as she ate her chow mein. Callie tried to make it as brief an explanation as possible but she realized if she left too much out, it wouldn't make any sense.

"So," said Mom when Callie had finished, "do you feel it was worthwhile to go speak to them?"

"I think so, but who knows? It's hard to tell from looking at people's faces."

"True, but do you feel they were an attentive group overall?" Callie wondered what her mother was getting at.

"I spose."

"Well, the reason I'm asking is that this might've been a good experience in terms of choosing a career, such as teaching. If you felt comfortable and you held their attention, it could indicate your suitability for particular types of career choices. Of course, one time won't tell you the answer, but it could be an indication."

"Mom, I've got a while before I decide on a career."

"Of course you do, dear. I'm not trying to rush you out the door," Mom laughed.

"Sheesh!" exclaimed Callie in mock indignation. "A person could get the feeling they're not wanted."

"Oh, you're wanted all right. Who'd help with chores otherwise?" quipped Dad, grinning.

"Daaaaadd," replied Callie. But that's what she liked about her family. They kept things light. Not always. But Dad said there was enough serious stuff in the world that you'd go crazy just focusing on that. A little humor made the ride less bumpy, he'd say. Well, she didn't know if life was a ride but she knew life would be a whole lot harder without Jesus. Dad believed Jesus had a sense of humor, and set an example for us too. Still, Callie hadn't seen too much of that humor in the Bible, but Dad reminded her that the Bible wasn't provided as a joke book, but matters of life and death. Still, he maintained that you could find humor within its pages if you looked for it. He reminded her that even in its earliest chapters a person could find the lightheartedness in the animals God had created. The giraffe was an example with its long – yet practical – neck. That neck could reach up to the leaves on the high branches. Callie remembered her first visit to the zoo and craning her own neck just to see the giraffe's head. Skunks and porcupines might be funny too – but only from a distance. Dad had said there was a certain humor to be found in the pride of man who, throughout the Bible, proved how foolish mortals can be. God, although He provided humans with free will, ultimately has power over all. When humans challenge Him and His power, they learn a sad and sorry – although valuable – lesson. Callie respected her father's wisdom and experience.

CHAPTER NINE

Now with Christmas approaching, Callie thought about the United Home School Group of Pine Moor and the Christmas Pageant they'd be presenting. She enjoyed getting together with her fellow home school students, especially at this time of year. It had really become quite the local event in Pine Moor. Young and old attended and took it all in with gusto. This year Callie even had the task, if one could call it that, of selecting carols to be used as well as to help with the set and stage preparations. They would be having the nativity scene featuring the latest newborn in the combined congregations as the Baby Jesus. This year it would be little Timothy Hanley who was just a month and a half old. If he could be well-fed and newly diapered, he might just sleep through the scene. If not, everyone would understand for the short time he'd spend in the manger that George Lang had crafted for that purpose. It was bound to be an enjoyable evening all the way around.

Callie discussed the Pageant at church with Sarah Jo. The planning was half the fun.

"I can hardly wait to see the costumes for the village scene," said Sarah Jo. "I mean we set up one of those villages – like the town square - every year on the buffet in the dining room at our house. It looks so real you just wish you could be there."

"I know," agreed Callie. "They look so quaint. Our skit will bring home the real meaning of Christmas."

"Yep – if no one forgets their lines," giggled Sarah Jo. "Thankfully, it's a short skit; direct and to the point."

"I wonder how Riley Woodboro will do as Pastor Jackson when he leads the carolers," said Callie.

"I don't know, but I've heard him sing and he's not half bad."

"Well, it sure would be funny if he was leading the carolers but couldn't carry a tune in a bucket," laughed Callie.

"That's why Donnie Maxwell was turned down. He can't sing," asserted Sarah Jo.

"Oh well," added Callie. "He sorta looks like the pastor type." She was surprised to find a small envelope addressed to her in the mail box on Tuesday when she went to get the mail after lunch. There was no return address. She opened up the envelope and pulled out the card that said Thank You on the front in script. On the inside the handwritten message said:

Dear Callie,

I just want to thank you again for the helpful presentation you put on for our school age children. That, along with answering questions, has filled in the blanks for a lot of us unfamiliar with home school. I hope to see you soon.

Peace, Fern Samuels

She hoped to see her *soon?* Why? There really was no reason to, thought Callie. Armed with that knowledge, she'd make a point of being unavailable. Now, with winter fast approaching, Callie would be indoors most of the time anyway. What was it with this woman? Oh well, maybe it was just an expression. People said "See you soon" all the time. That's probably what that Samuels woman meant.

In the meantime, Callie had some major studying to do. The end of the quarter was approaching and she'd be having exams. A lot of that was based on trust since technically she could cheat and look up the answers one way or the other, but her home school provider had an adage: *Cheating only cheats you in the end.* Besides, what was the point in getting an education that you have to pay for only to waste it? The phone rang and she noticed by caller ID that it was Wendy.

"Hey Wendy, what's up? Haven't heard from you in a while."

"Hi Callie. I just thought I'd give you a quick call. Nobody's home here and, as you probably know, there's teachers conferences today and tomorrow," said Wendy

"Yeh, I know," replied Callie. "I'm using the time to study anyway – with exams coming up. How's school going for you?" At that point a call waiting came through for Callie. She debated whether she should take it, but it might be Mom. "Hang on a sec, Wendy." Callie pushed the button. "Hello?"

"Hi Callie, this is Fern Samuels. How are you today, dear?"

"Actually, I'm on another call. Can I call you back?"

"This will only take a moment, dear." Before she could protest, Mrs. Samuels continued, "I recall you mentioning something about a heaven club? Well, curiosity has simply gotten the best of me. I must know more." Callie scrambled to think of what to say.

"Well, I couldn't possibly explain all that now. Maybe you could call our pastor though. He - "

"No, Callie, I'd prefer you explain it to me. How would it be if we met at the Pine Moor Coffee Post like maybe tomorrow at, say, two o'clock." Callie noted by Mrs. Samuels' tone of voice that it wasn't a question but, rather, a statement. She wondered what Wendy must be thinking at this point as she waited for Callie to get back. So she agreed, just to end this call with Mrs. Samuels.

"Good dear. I'll see you tomorrow at two then."

*****

"Hey, what happened to you?" asked Wendy.

"Oh nothing. Just this lady who calls me from time to time. She came to our house on the first day of school."

"What did she want?"

"I guess to just give me some free magazines," said Callie.

"That's weird," declared Wendy. "So, how did you get to know her?"

"Well, her little girl needed to use the bathroom, so I let them in. Otherwise no one's sposed to come in the house when my parents aren't here."

"Oh, and so she got in a conversation with you?"

"Something like that," replied Callie. "Hey, I don't want to talk about her anymore. What's going on with you?

"Not too much. School's kind of a drag but I keep telling myself that I'm supposed to be a light there."

"How's Laura doing?"

"She's okay," said Wendy. "She's kinda got a boyfriend, but she'd prob'ly say he's just a friend."

"Hmmm. Has she been going to the Heaven Club meetings?" asked Callie.

"She hasn't missed one yet," explained Wendy.

"Hey, good for her," commended Callie. "Well, maybe you can get together with her once in awhile. Get her mind off guys. If she gets involved with one, it might lead her down a wrong path."

"Yeh, I know. The guys around here only have one thing on their mind – girls!"

"Not just guys *there* – pretty much everywhere." They both laughed.

Rehearsals for the pageant were going well. At least Callie thought so, and she heard no complaints from any of the parents who were helping out. The stage, especially the quaint village set, looked very real. In the distance painted skaters on a pond "enjoyed" their blissful – and graceful - pastime. Callie had found a very talented student from their home school group to do specific artwork. Luke Mathews wanted to go to art school or so he'd told her, but the cost was prohibitive. So, anything he could do to add to his portfolio even now would be helpful, he'd admitted. She was glad to accommodate his desire to contribute in an artistic way.

Those kids on the pond looked life-like.

They also had arranged for artificial snow to be a part of the scene. That would be handled from above by stage hands. It was rather ironic since there already was an abundant supply of snow outside, but just not practical for the purpose of the pageant. It would put people in the mood though. Things were looking good, admitted Callie.

The next day Callie kept her word and went to the Pine Moor Coffee Post as she'd agreed to. Mrs. Samuels was already there, waiting.

"Hello Callie, dear," Mrs. Samuels said. "I held off ordering until you got here. I wasn't sure what you wanted. Maybe some hot chocolate on such a cold day?"

"Uh, sure, that'll be fine."

"Good. I'll be right back." Mrs. Samuels got up from the booth and hurried off to the counter. She returned almost immediately with steaming hot coffee for herself and a cup of hot cocoa for Callie. "By the way, dear, just so you know, this coffee is decaf. We don't drink the high-powered stuff." Callie figured the "we" she referred to were the members of her church - or maybe just her own family.

"Thank you," said Callie as Mrs. Samuels placed the hot mug of cocoa in front of her.

"You're more than welcome, dear," replied Mrs. Samuels. "It'll taste good on a day like today." She took a sip of coffee as if to see how hot it was. "Mmmm.. this tastes good too. So Callie, you mentioned something about a heaven club. I'm interested. Just what is it?"

"It's a group of teens from our church who want to learn about heaven. So we formed a club. Actually, four of us started the club, but the other two girls are from Addison."

"Oh, so then you are all friends," concluded Mrs. Samuels.

"Yes, we are."

"How nice. So do you get together often?"

"We hold the Heaven Club once a month here at our church, like on a Saturday," said Callie.

"I see. So, what is discussed at your meetings?"

"Well, we sometimes read books about NDE, uh, near death experience, and share with the others. Or sometimes Pastor reads right from the Bible."

"Hmmm... I wouldn't think near death experiences would be very reliable. I mean you're just taking someone's word for it."

"What these people have been through is very real to them," explained Callie.

"Yes, but the Bible is the only reliable source of information on this subject," reminded Mrs. Samuels.

"True, but you might say that there were people in the Bible who experienced an NDE. Even Jesus arose from the dead."

"Callie! I'd caution you to be careful when bringing our Lord into this," admonished Mrs. Samuels who now had a disapproving look on her face. Callie felt uncomfortable. She didn't need anyone to explain things like that to her.

"I'm just telling you what we do at the meetings is all. And those are the things we talk about," said Callie.

"Have you ever thought about the fact that there are so many religions? They can't all be right," declared the older woman.

"I don't think anyone said they were," returned Callie. "It's just there are quite a few denominations. They all hold to the basic tenets of faith."

"Do they, Callie- do they really?"

"Well, the ones I know of do."

"You might want to do a little research on the subject. You might be surprised, dear."

"Maybe there is no perfect religion, Mrs. Samuels."

"Don't be so quick to dismiss the subject, Callie. Of course there is."

"All I know is where it says 'Pure religion is to visit the fatherless and widows in their affliction'" said Callie. "I think it's in James."

"That would be 'Pure religion and undefiled before God and the Father is this, To visit the fatherless and widows in their affliction, and to keep himself unspotted from the world.' That's James chapter one, verse twenty-seven."

"I was close," said Callie defensively. "At least I had the right book of the Bible."

"Callie, my dear, how wrong you are. When it comes to the Bible, close doesn't count. You have to be, how do they put it? Spot on; yes, right on target. No room for varying or degrees."

"Mrs. Samuels, if I may ask, what does this have to do with the Heaven Club?"

"Everything Callie, as you will see, if you'll but keep an open mind. Otherwise, how does one learn?"

"Well, I think I'd better finish up here and get home. I have things to do," said Callie, setting her jaw.

"Don't leave just yet," ordered Mrs. Samuels. "I'm not finished. I think you'll want to hear what I have to say. I mean you don't want to lose your salvation, do you? It could happen if you're too stubborn to hear the truth."

"Jesus said, 'thy word is truth.'"

"Callie, you don't have to preach the Bible to me. I'm a lot older than you and I know where that *partial* verse you quoted is from. But you make my point. Man's opinion compared to the Bible - or about the Bible - means less than nothing."

"A lot of people have written books about Bible things," said Callie.

"That's true, dear, but that doesn't mean they're right, does it?"

"Uh, I don't know. I guess not." Callie was feeling confused. It was the first step toward questioning her own beliefs.

CHAPTER TEN

The Pageant was a smashing success according to Rhonda Blair from Dad's work. Someone from the *Community Times,* Pine Moor's weekly community newspaper, had asked her opinion as attendees flocked out after the performance. A light snow was dusting sidewalks and streets like powdered sugar falling from the sky. Inside the theater, which was a grand old edifice built years ago and where many productions had taken place, Callie was checking to make sure everything was done that needed to be before leaving for the night. Of course, she wasn't really in charge of everything; Mr. Knight would be locking up when everyone had vacated the building. But she did her part on making sure that things moved along at a fairly speedy pace so as not to keep him there any longer than necessary. The set would be dismantled on the weekend when there would be ample help. Costumes would be stored away for next year. The cavernous old theater had plenty of room for storage of such costumes – plus many more as Callie had noted while in the wardrobe area, which smelled of moth balls.

"Hey Callie," called out Sarah Jo from backstage. "I know you're here somewhere."

"Yes, I'm right here," she answered as she peeped out from a doorway. "I'm just making sure everything is put away where it belongs."

"You did a great job this year, Cal."

"You weren't so bad yourself. I really liked your solo during caroling."

"Speaking of which," added Sarah Jo, "Riley really outdid himself as a minister."

"Wow! Did he ever!" agreed Callie as she stooped to pick up an ink pen someone had dropped. "Maybe that's his calling in life." For some reason, that struck both girls as funny and they giggled. Someone stuck their head in the doorway.

"Hey Callie, good job tonight." It was Mrs. Samuels. That woman is *everywhere* – at least everywhere *I* am, thought Callie.

"Thank you," Callie answered hastily. Then remembering her manners she added, "this is my friend Sarah Jo Foster."

"How lovely to meet you," returned Mrs. Samuels as she extended her hand.

"Same here," responded Sarah Jo.

"Well, I'd better get moving," said Mrs. Samuels. "Now, where's Olivia? *Olivia!* Where are you?" There was a look of exasperation on Mrs. Samuels' face as she turned on her heel to leave. Callie and Sarah Jo looked at each other and shrugged.

"I spose we'd better go help her find her daughter," said Sarah Jo.

"That's for sure! She could be anywhere in this big old theater." Finally, a half an hour later Olivia was found crouching behind one of the huge potted ferns on its marble pedestal near the reception hall at the entrance of the theater. The little girl was crying and ran to her mother who wrapped her arms around her.

"We were looking *all over* for you, Olivia Jean!"

"But mama," said Olivia haltingly through her sobs. "I saw a ghost back there!"

"Olivia Jean! You know we don't believe in such things. Your father will have to punish you for what you did tonight."

"No mama," pleaded the girl. "I saw one. It was white and scary!"

"My word, don't act like such a little baby!"

Callie was embarrassed for Olivia. She knew that discipline was important but not shaming her like that. A thought came to her.

"Mrs. Samuels, I think I might be able to help."

"I'm not sure how you can help a girl with a wild imagination like Olivia has," answered Mrs. Samuels curtly.

"I think I might. Everyone come with me. It's okay, Olivia. Your mom is right here with you." They made their way to the back of the theater, Sarah Jo as well. Backstage, there was a door slightly ajar.

"I'm afraid, mama," whined Olivia.

"Did you go in this door, Olivia?" Callie pointed to the sewing room as it was referred to – the place where last minute alterations could be made on the various costumes. Olivia nodded.

"What does this have to do with anything?" asked a perturbed Mrs. Samuels. "It's late and my daughter needs to go to bed." Callie squatted down on Olivia's level and looked into the little girl's teary eyes.

"I'm going to show you what you *thought* looked like a ghost and prove to you that there's no way it could be. Your mom will hold your hand," said Callie as she noted the white knuckled grip the little girl had on her mother's hand. "Now, don't be afraid. I'm not." Callie stepped in the room. Olivia, at her mother's side, followed hesitantly.

"This is what scared you, Olivia, but as you can see it's nothing but a dress form with a white sheet over it to keep the dust off."

"Open your eyes, Olivia," commanded her mother. "See how foolish you've been about this whole thing." Callie removed the sheet to reveal the form beneath.

"Here's how it helps us," explained Callie. She took a vest from a table and put it on the form. "See?" The little girl finally nodded, which satisfied her mother.

"Come along, Olivia," said Mrs. Samuels. "We're going home now." Without so much as a word of good bye or wave of the hand, the two were on their way to the main entrance.

"Sheesh!" exclaimed Sarah Jo. "So that's the lady that had you speak to the kids about home school a couple weeks ago?"

"Yep," replied Callie. "Nice lady, huh? Even *I* didn't know she treated her daughter like that."

"Well, it's not exactly a crime, but it's not going to help her daughter any – especially her, let's see, I think the big term is self-esteem," said Sarah Jo. "I don't think she'd like it if God treated *her* that way; the mom, that is."

"That's for sure. Well, I spose we'd better get going. Mr. Knight looks like he's ready to lock up."

"You girls finished here?" he asked.

"Yes," they answered in unison. Sarah Jo's parents were waiting outside the theater for the girls.

"My goodness!" exclaimed Mrs. Foster. "It sure took you awhile to finish what you were doing."

"It's not Sarah Jo's fault," said Callie. "A lady I know lost her daughter in the theater and we had to find her."

"Who is that?" inquired Sarah Jo's father.

"Her name is Fern Samuels. Her little girl Olivia got scared when she wandered away from her mother."

"Nope. Never heard of her. She's from around here?"

"I guess so. I don't know where they live," said Callie. Her parents were home by the time the Fosters dropped her off.

"Hi dear," greeted Mom when Callie walked in the door.

"So – what did you think? Did you like the Pageant?" asked Callie as she removed her snowy shoes by the door.

"Oh yes!" answered Mom enthusiastically. "Your group outdid themselves this year."

"I'd say," concurred Dad. "I thought that Riley Woodbury –"

"Woodboro," corrected Callie.

"Well, I thought he was a hoot. When he cracked that joke, the audience could hardly contain themselves."

"Oh, you mean when he asked the quartet if they were merry and ready to carol?" asked Callie.

"Yes," said Dad, "then the kid added, 'Or are you Carol and ready to be merry?'"

"Daddd..." said Callie in an exasperated tone of voice. "That was so corny, it could've filled a silo. His mic shouldn't have even caught that."

"Well anyway, *I* thought it was funny," declared Dad, as he reached for the remote to turn on the late night news.

*****

Christmas was just days away and Callie was glad to be caught up in the hustle and bustle of the holiday. The family would be staying home this year. Dad said fuel prices were prohibitive to do any kind of long distance travel. Besides, he'd said, the weather was so unpredictable. After her recently unenjoyable encounters with Mrs. Samuels, Callie wouldn't have minded leaving town. That way there'd be no chance of running into her. It didn't take long before that unfortunate – at least in Callie's mind – eventuality took place close to home and unexpectedly, as usual.

Callie was shopping for a gift for Dad at one of the local sporting goods stores. She supposed she could've shopped online but she liked the idea of seeing what she was getting *before* she bought it. Dad wasn't easy to shop for.

*****

"Well hello, Callie," came an all too familiar voice from the next aisle. "I *thought* that was you."

"Hi, Mrs. Samuels," replied Callie less than enthusiastically. Callie put down the football jersey she'd been looking at.

"How's Callie today?" asked Mrs. Samuels as she joined her.

"Doing okay, I guess."

"Just okay? I'm surprised. The Christian life ought to make us ecstatically happy," said the buoyant Mrs. Samuels. "Is something wrong?"

"No, I'm just doing some shopping for my parents."

"Oh, well maybe I can help you then," said Mrs. Samuels. "I think you're in the wrong store though. You should check the book store down the block. They have a spiritual book section that has some good reads in there. A Bible is usually a safe choice."

"My father already has one," said Callie.

"Oh, you can never have too many," said Mrs. Samuels. "We have more than a few in our home. We leave them throughout the house, open." Callie smiled weakly and wished that either she or Mrs. Samuels hadn't come to this store.

"Are you finding what you're looking for?" asked a well-groomed teenage boy with a name tag that said: Clint.

"Well, I was just telling Callie here –"

"Um, I'd better get going. There's some place I have to be," declared Callie.

Any place but *here!* she thought in a panic. She didn't want this perfect stranger to know the story of her life, compliments of Mrs. Samuels.

"Good bye, dear," Mrs. Samuels called after her. Callie didn't bother with a goodbye, but rather, escaped out the door as if a rabid dog was in hot pursuit.

She was out of breath by the time she reached her street. She almost thought if she looked behind her, there Mrs. Samuels would be. Was she stalking her or something? No, thought Callie, these were just chance encounters. Still, there was something eerie about it.

The house was empty upon her arrival. Even though she had off from school, work was still on for her parents. She decided to give Sarah Jo a call on the outside chance that she would be home and not out shopping like she had just been.

"Sarah Jo? Hi, this is Callie."

"Hi Cal, what's up?"

"That's what I'd like to know," answered Callie. "I keep running into Mrs. Samuels – or the other way around. It's getting creepy."

"In what way?" asked Sarah Jo.

"It's like every time I turn around, she's there. Like she's following me or something."

"I think you've been reading the wrong books or something, Cal. Why would she be following you?"

"I don't know," said Callie. Then she went on to explain what had happened earlier.

"A lot of people go into different stores at this time of year," said Sarah Jo. "You're bound to run into people you know."

"Maybe so, but it's like she's trying to tell me what to do. I hardly know her," complained Callie. "It's not like I asked for her help."

"Well, I'll pray about it – you should too. Maybe God is showing you something."

"Yeh, like to not ever open the door to strangers." The two girls chuckled, but Callie was still uncomfortable.

CHAPTER ELEVEN

The new year came in with a literal bang. Pine Moor might be small, but they took their holidays seriously. So even though there was snow on the ground, the sky was clear. Fireworks were set off at the fair grounds, although not so numerous as the Fourth of July. It was just a reminder that the new year held hope for greater things. Callie sure hoped it did, although the previous year had been pretty good.

At least she hadn't run into Mrs. Samuels since that encounter in the sporting goods store and, no, she didn't buy a Bible for her father for Christmas; and yes, she had purchased a football jersey for him which he put on immediately. Mom teased him and called him the pajama quarterback and they all laughed. Dad returned the favor when he presented her with a box so heavy it defied explanation. It was rather long and flat with no rattle or clue as to what was within. Mom had a captive audience when she finally got past the wrappings and down to the box that when opened revealed an iron skillet in the shape of their state.

"What's this?" she asked wide-eyed.

"My love, this is what my breakfast will be cooked in today," answered Dad.

"Well, it will have to be seasoned first," reminded Mom as she searched for the information on it.

"I'm not sure, but it might be pre-seasoned," said Dad. "By the way, just so you don't think there's a method to my madness I also have this for you. He produced an envelope from where it had been hidden within the branches of the tree.

"Bruce, I love it! I would never have thought of going to a spa on my own, but this gift certificate will be my ticket to paradise for a couple of hours."

Callie had given Mom a bottle of her favorite perfume. Callie herself had been lavished with gifts from Mom and Dad, one of which was an eReader which they reminded her was not to take the place of actual hold-in-your-hand books.

*****

Callie immersed herself in her studies and church as well as the Heaven Club. Life was beginning to show promise in terms of blessings, not so much of material things but of achievements and small investments in her future. She knew she must not waste precious time on foolishness as she'd seen other girls her age do. If she wanted to make something of herself, or more importantly if God did, she needed to be preparing right now. It all came to a screeching halt one blustery March afternoon. The phone rang and without thinking, Callie answered.

"Hi," said a child's voice.

"Who's calling, please?" asked Callie.

"Hello?" asked the voice.

"Hello," said Callie, this time with emphasis. "Who's calling?"

"Hello," said an adult voice, a familiar one. "Callie, is that you?"

"Mrs. Samuels?"

"Yes, it's me. I'm so sorry. Olivia must've pressed speed dial for your number. Sometimes she goes into my purse."

"Oh," said Callie, not knowing how to respond. Mom never let her go into her purse for any reason. She always said that it belonged to her and that she was to respect others' things. Callie had been taught to bring the purse to her mother and she'd get whatever it was from there.

"Well, now that I have you on the phone, I'd like to ask you something," said Mrs. Samuels.

"Uh.. okay," answered Callie.

"Have you given any thought to what I told you at the coffee shop? People often hold as true things that are not simply because they've been taught wrongly."

"I don't know what you mean," said Callie. She wished that she could just hang up on Mrs. Samuels, but she would never do that.

"How do you know what you believe to be true is actually true?"

"The Bible says so," said Callie.

"There are Bibles and there are Bibles," declared Mrs. Samuels firmly.

"Huh?"

"You heard me right, Callie. Have you heard of the Alvin Barton Translation of the Holy Scriptures?"

"No, I haven't." Who was *Alvin Barton?*

"In some circles, that is considered to be the most accurate translation of the Bible," proclaimed Mrs. Samuels.

"It is?" asked Callie. "I've never heard of it."

"Well, that doesn't make it any less true though. I have an extra one. Would you like me to drop it off at your house?" asked Mrs. Samuels.

"I'm really busy today. I've got a paper to write and submit before the end of the week."

"Well, I'll tell you what. I have an errand to run today. I'll just drop it off on your front porch this afternoon. That way I won't be disturbing you. How does that sound?"

"I guess that'll be okay," responded Callie. "About what time will you drop it off?"

"Probably between one and two o'clock."

"Okay."

*****

One thing about Mrs. Samuels, Callie found, she always kept her word. The Bible was in a plastic bag right outside the front door. Callie brought it in and gave it a cursory inspection – just enough to notice that it looked no different than any other Bible, except that it wasn't leather-bound or fancy in any way. Upon opening its cover, Callie saw a dedication that said:

Dedicated to all my fervent students of the Bible. Let us all humble ourselves and learn from the Word of God. II Timothy 2.15

Callie knew that verse well since she'd heard it many times at church.

It said: "Be diligent to present yourself approved to God, a worker who does not need to be ashamed, rightly dividing the word of truth." She didn't have time to look at that Bible now though. She needed to get back to writing her paper. Although her concentration had been interrupted, she got back into the flow of the theme of it. History was not one of her favorite subjects, mainly because she believed much of it had been tampered with. That was specifically what she was writing about. The thing was, she found it hard to disprove what the history books had recorded, so it meant she must research even more deeply on the internet.

"Hi dear," called out Mom from the front door where she'd just entered.

"How's your schoolwork coming along?"

"Pretty good, I guess," answered Callie. Mom poked her head in the office doorway. "I'm kind of getting bogged down though."

"Maybe you should take a break," suggested Mom. "It'll refresh your mind. Want some tea?"

"Sure," answered Callie. "That sounds good." She got up from the computer and followed her mother into the kitchen. "Do you want me to make it?"

"That's okay," answered Mom. "I'll be the servant today. Work was a breeze for some reason. I think everyone's still happy from the holidays." She placed a couple of mugs on the table. "Regular tea or herbal?"

"I think I'll have some mint tea, Mom. Thanks." The tea kettle whistled urgently on the stove. Soon mother and daughter were sipping tea and making small talk. Then Callie blurted out a question.

"Mom, which do you think is the best Bible to use?"

"*Best?*" I don't know if I'd rate them according to best. Each translation has pluses and minuses."

"Like what?" asked Callie as she set her mug down.

"Well, for example, many people feel the King James version of the Bible is very accurate. However, it's written in the rather stilted language of its day. I mean Jesus didn't use words like thee or thou when he was talking to someone. It would be like I would say: 'Would you bring thy Bible to me?' It is said that Jesus spoke Aramaic. However, his words were translated into the language of the translators' day which for the King James version was early modern during that Elizabethan period."

"So, does that make it inaccurate?" asked Callie.

"Well, not necessarily, but it's nice to have other translations to compare with. Your father has a parallel Bible that he occasionally refers to. It contains other translations."

"Wow – I suppose there are quite a few versions then," noted Callie.

"Unfortunately, some of the more modern versions of the Bible indicate that the translators have taken liberties they ought not have. But that's where studying comes in as well as other Biblical study aids come in. God doesn't hold a person accountable for what he or she *doesn't* know, but rather what they do know. But it's up to that person to at least crack open the Bible to investigate, kind of like the Bereans. Do you remember that verse?"

"Wasn't it about them searching the Scriptures daily to prove what was true?"

"Yes, it's in Acts 17:11 which says: 'Be diligent to present yourself approved to God, a worker who does not need to be ashamed, rightly dividing the word of truth.' It's the principle of checking scripture to make sure it says what what you've heard or been told, from whatever source," said Mom.

"Makes sense to me. That's kind of what my paper is about regarding history."

"Well, you've bitten off a mouthful on that one, but if you can even find one or two incidents that make your point, you can save yourself a lot of time," said Mom.

"Hey, that's a good idea! I like that approach," agreed. Callie. She finished her tea and dug in to research on the computer again. When she was finished for the day, she had come close to uncovering a battle during the Civil War that had some questionable information swirling around it. She would look into it further tomorrow.

Later that evening, Callie decided to look at the Bible Mrs. Samuels had left for her. That way if Mrs. Samuels called and asked if she'd looked at it, she could say yes without lying, which she knew was wrong. Besides that, she felt rather curious about it since she'd asked Mom about various translations of the Bible earlier. There was a table of contents in the front with all the books of the Bible listed in proper order, just as with any Bible. But wait! What was this book right before Acts? The Lost Gospel of Ambrose. She'd never heard of that. It wasn't in *her* Bible. She wondered what it was about and turned there. It started out:

In the times and seasons of the Great King, a proclamation was sent out in the land. Many people were subject to the great Power of the King of the land. It was at this time that the Angel of Power exerted no less than all of his influence far and wide.

What sense did that make? thought Callie. It seemed like there was a hidden message, but she had no idea what it was. For that matter, she really didn't care to know.

"Callie, can you help me with dinner?" called Mom from the kitchen.

"Sure Mom."

"Here, take these green beans and wash them and cut them up. I just happened to find fresh ones in the store. I don't know where they brought them in from, but they sounded good."

"Hey Mom, have you ever heard of a guy in the Bible named Ambrose?"

"Not that I know of. Doesn't sound familiar. Why?" Callie didn't want to get into it with Mom. That would mean talking about Mrs. Samuels and she didn't feel like thinking about her right now.

"Oh nothing. I was just wondering."

CHAPTER TWELVE

It seemed silly to Callie that Sarah Jo wanted to hold a young people's Bible study at the Fosters' home. Maybe not literally silly, but unnecessary seeing as how they held regular Bible studies at church.

"So, what's your reason for wanting to do this, Sarah Jo?"

"I thought it would be a good way for teens – girls and guys – to get together for something uplifting, or as Pastor says, edifying. It's not going to be heavy duty or anything," replied Sarah Jo.

"So, who's in charge?"

"Well, Mom and Dad talked to Pastor Martin about it and he felt it would be a good idea to let us young people conduct it ourselves, with one parent – it will be my mom – supervising."

"I don't know, Sarah Jo. I've never heard of doing it that way before."

"Well, the thing is, Pastor Martin felt it would be great leadership training as well as to have peer interaction."

"Who's going to be in charge the first time?" asked Callie.

"You wanna be?"

"No way! I'll come, but I don't want to be in charge."

"Which is *exactly* why you need this, Cal. But relax, I'll be in charge of the first one."

"*First?* You mean there's gonna be more?" asked Callie, wide-eyed.

"If it works out well, then why not? Kids our age need something to do that's more than slow dancing together or hanging out at a big mall."

"Well, we don't have one of those here, Sarah Jo. Prob'ly never will."

"You know what I mean, Cal. It's good to have a get-together with girls and guys where one or the other isn't the focus like with regular dating. Here, God will be the focus. I think it'll bring out the best in us for everyone to see and get to know."

Callie was pleasantly surprised to find that to be true. There were ten people in attendance; Mrs. Foster made eleven. And oddly, Riley Woodboro showed up as well as Donnie Maxwell. Riley sat across from Callie, while Donnie sat next to her on the couch. She felt self-conscious at first but soon everyone was involved in the discussion except for Mrs. Foster who sat there listening to the group.

"There's a lot written about Jesus in the Bible," said Sarah Jo. "But there's also much that isn't. So do you think He had the same feelings that we as teens do now?"

"Well, I think if we were meant to know that, it would be in the Bible," said Annie Hopkins whose tiny voice matched her frame.

"Huh?" asked Riley. Annie repeated what she'd said, this time louder.

"A lot of what we know is based on the principles that He taught," said Donnie.

"Yeh, like how He was tempted in all ways like we are," added Riley.

"But Jesus didn't go out on dates and stuff like teens today do," argued Callie.

"I'd like to remind everyone that back in Jesus' time, young people got married at a young age, so that kind of thing was taken seriously," added Mrs. Foster.

"So, why didn't He get married?" asked Donnie. No one answered.

"Well, we knew He was on a mission," said Sarah Jo. "But marriage wasn't it – at least not physical marriage as we know it."

"Why didn't His parents arrange for him to marry?" asked Lydia Drew.

"Well, His mother, Mary, knew He was sent from God," said LeAnne Migalski, an older teen who was almost as tall as Riley.

"Good point, LeAnne," said Sarah Jo.

"We don't even know if Jesus wanted to get married or even court someone," added Annie. "The Bible doesn't tell us much about His life other than His birth and the three years up till when He died – and then information about His return."

"Well, I don't think we should fill in the blanks about those things," said Lydia.

"I agree," Callie heard herself commenting. "I mean everything's in the Bible that we're meant to know, right?"

"Excuse me, Sarah Jo," said Mrs. Foster. "I'd like to add a comment that might be helpful."

"Sure Mom," answered Sarah Jo.

"Well, I have to wonder if we're looking at this too much from the human perspective. We have to remember that the spiritual trumps the physical. Yes, Jesus was both God and man, but He came down from heaven to be our Saviour.

And yes, we are to be the collective Bride of Christ and there will be the wedding between Him and His people. So, in a way, *that* marriage takes precedence over human marriage. Although human marriage is very important, *this* marriage that takes place between the Bridegroom Jesus and His people is in the spiritual realm. You might say that human marriage was designed after the heavenly one." The teens nodded.

"That makes sense," concurred Sarah Jo. "It's interesting that the Parable of the Ten Virgins in Matthew 25 used the comparison of marriage to the return of Jesus Christ, the Bridegroom."

"Yes, but I think the original question was did Jesus have the same feelings teens do today, and did He date?" asked Annie.

"I'd say yes, and no," replied Callie. "He had feelings like we do, but He didn't date like teens do today. He probably was too busy helping Joseph and also learning like when He was in the temple at age twelve that time."

"It's a good question," added Mrs. Foster, "but, once again, I have to say we mustn't try to focus on the man Jesus, but on Jesus as God who was obedient to the Father's plan. Any comments?" There were.

After discussing if and when they'd like to meet again, they needed little coaxing to help themselves to refreshments. Sarah Jo sat down next to Callie on the couch.

"So, what do you think? Do you think things went well tonight?" asked Sarah Jo.

"I think they did," answered Callie as she nibbled on a snickerdoodle. "Why? What do you think?"

"I guess it went well enough. The subject was sort of tricky though, as my dad would say," said Sarah Jo.

"Tricky?" asked Callie.

"Well, I kind of picked it so that everyone would think – a subject that's relevant to us."

"Good call, SJ," confirmed Callie.

"Hey ladies," announced Donnie as he inserted himself in the space between Callie and the arm of the couch. "Do you mind?"

"Does it matter?" shot back Sarah Jo, laughing. She was used to his clowning around and she couldn't resist a quick comeback.

"Yes, it *matters*," he answered with mock concern. "If you mind, it makes it all worthwhile."

"Silly!" declared Sarah Jo as she threw a couch pillow in his direction. They all laughed.

"Hey, what's going on here?" asked Riley as he sauntered up to the couch with a brownie in one hand, a glass of milk in the other.

"Aw, I was just teasing Sarah Jo here," confessed Donnie.

"So, what did you think of this Bible study, Riley?" asked Sarah Jo.

"Hey, it has its merits," he replied. "I learned something anyway."

"What's that, big guy?" asked Donnie.

"Well, for one thing, how young they got married back then," answered Riley.

"And the other?" asked Callie as she tried to put a little more distance between her and Donnie on the couch.

"Hey, I can take a hint," said Donnie with mock hurt feelings. "I'm crushed."

"So was I - literally," retorted Callie.

"What were you going to say, Riley?" asked Sarah Jo.

"Well, I guess I didn't realize how important marriage is to God," explained Riley. "I mean we just take it for granted that it's a way of life. You grow up and get married and stuff. But God sees it on a whole spiritual level."

"These days a lot of people don't even bother with marriage," said Sarah Jo.

"I think that's dumb," said Donnie. "I mean if a guy and a girl live together without being married, what if they have a kid or something?"

"Yeh, not to mention that if one little thing ticks off one of them, they can bail on the relationship, no questions asked," said Riley.

"So, you guys believe in marriage, huh?" asked Lydia who'd been standing nearby.

"Sure, why not?" answered Donnie. "But it's not in my future for a long time."

"Well, if it got around school that you *do* believe in it, you'd prob'ly get laughed out of the place," said Lydia. "Not that I'm against marriage. Just sayin'."

"Well, I care more about what God thinks than what people think," added Donnie. He got up from the couch.

"Bravo!" extolled Mrs. Foster, clapping. "I had hoped a Bible study like this would open up dialogue. We learn from the Bible, but also from one another."

Upon her arrival home, Callie's parents were at no loss for questions about the Bible study. When she'd answered them all, her mother said she'd give Annie and some of the others a ride home next time, just as Annie's mother had for Callie.

"I'm so in favor of a Bible study like this – and it sounds like it really worked out well."

"It did, Mom. We had a good time – and learned stuff too."

"Great," chimed in Dad. "That's good to hear."

Callie was happy and relieved to learn that her history report which she'd emailed in got a B+. A notation in red on it said: *Hard to grade, but nicely presented.* It was worth all the hours of research she had put into it. Not only that, but Mom and Dad were pleased.

Easter, or Resurrection Sunday as their church referred to it, was just around the corner. Although she knew the tradition behind the day, which had mostly to do with eggs and rabbits – both symbolic of bringing life into the world – her focus was on what Jesus Christ had done for her and all the world in giving His life. The gospel message to her was like a banner carried in battle; it always reminded the warrior of the Cause. She figured His cross was the spiritual banner. Her love of history had made her curious as to why in the midst of battle brave men would be the standard bearers of the country they were willing to die for. She found out that the flag was all-important to the troops in battle that the flag that embodied all they'd put their life on the line for was still there for them to see.

Her phone rang and thinking it might be Sarah Jo, she answered it without looking first to see who it was calling.

"Hello, Sarah Jo?"

"No, this is Mrs. Samuels – Fern Samuels. How are you today, dear?" Why didn't she check the screen first to see who was calling? Callie scolded herself inwardly.

"Oh, hi."

"I need some help on something and you were the first person I thought of," said Mrs. Samuels.

"Help with what?" asked Callie.

"Well, I sent for some home schooling materials and I'd hoped you could help me sift through some of these brochures and even sample packs."

"May I ask who they're for?"

"Well, basically the young people you spoke to about home school a while back," answered Mrs. Samuels. "Are you available tomorrow afternoon, being that it's Saturday?"

"Umm, let's see…" Callie hesitated. She hoped the Heaven Club would be meeting tomorrow, but no such luck if you could call it that. "I guess tomorrow's okay. What time and where?"

"How about at one o'clock at the same place where you spoke that time?"

"I guess that would be okay. I can't stay for too long though. I have some other things I have to do," said Callie.

"Oh, it won't take the whole afternoon, I'm sure. I'll see you then, Callie."

*****

Callie was glad for the short distance to meet with Mrs. Samuels. It had just begun misting out and, although it wasn't cold, she didn't feel like getting wet either.

Mrs. Samuels was seated at one long table on one side of the room, a stack of brochures piled neatly on one side.

"Hello, dear. Thank you so much for coming here to meet with me. Please sit down. Is it still drizzling out?"

"More like a mist," answered Callie as she draped her light jacket over the back of the folding chair.

"By the way, did you get a chance to look at the Bible I left you?" asked Mrs. Samuels casually.

"Not really in depth. I kind of just looked at the contents."

"Wonderful!" exclaimed Mrs. Samuels. "Alvin Barton was a very learned man. His Bible is an incredible testimony to what an individual can do when one applies him- or herself diligently. Although he translated many years ago what became this version of the Bible, it is very much relevant today."

"Well, like I said, I've never heard of him."

"That's a shame," clucked Mrs. Samuels. "Someone your age – well, all ages – could benefit from his teachings, and that Bible. It has answers to everyday problems."

"Maybe, but so does the Bible I have at home."

"Oh, but it's not like this one. Although Mr. Barton was raised in a very strict environment, it caused him to take his studies seriously. Plus, he had a problem with how arduous it was to read the Bible in King James English. So you won't find any of the 'thee' or 'thou' stilted language in it."

"Well, I also noticed there were other books of the Bible the King James doesn't include," said Callie. "And, by the way, there are other approved translations of the Bible that are more modern such as the New King James."

"Callie, I would rather have the most accurate version of the Bible and that would be the Alvin Barton Translation," asserted Mrs. Samuels. "Now, let's get to this information here, shall we?" Callie sifted through the many colorful pamphlets on the table before her. When they'd finished, Callie was reasonably certain that she'd been of help.

"Thank you so much, dear," said Mrs. Samuels as she gathered up the literature.

"You're welcome," answered Callie politely.

"Now, be sure to study that Bible I gave you. Notice I didn't say just read it." "Well uh.." stammered Callie.

"You need to learn about Jesus," ordered Mrs. Samuels. "You need to learn about what a good man he was, as well as a prophet, not to mention a man on the side of social revolution."

"*What?* Jesus is my Saviour," declared Callie.

"You may think so, but he was just a man. There was only so much he could do," asserted Mrs. Samuels.

"He is also God!" said Callie staunchly.

"You don't still believe that myth, do you dear?" questioned Mrs. Samuels. "That is so outdated. When you read Alvin Barton's Bible, you will see the truth for yourself."

Callie knew better than to argue with this woman and bid her a hasty good bye as she escaped out the door. As it shut behind her, Callie wondered what kind of a nut job Mrs. Samuels was. Just like with her history paper, she was going to prove Mrs. Samuels wrong. She couldn't do that in a back-and-forth argument; it would take research. First she must read what was in that Barton Bible.

CHAPTER THIRTEEN

Callie had plenty to do in the weeks ahead as she finished up the school year but, true to her resolve, she delved into that Alvin Barton Bible given to her by Mrs. Samuels. So far she had determined that much of the text contained in it matched up with the books in her own King James version. It was that Book of Ambrose that aroused her curiosity. Did someone named Ambrose actually write it? Was he a saint or someone of note? She could find nothing about him when she put that name in Search on her computer. All she came up with was a Saint Ambrose who was affiliated with a different church entirely. So, who *was* this man? She'd have to ask Mrs. Samuels, but she didn't want her to know that she was researching that Bible. She began to read farther into that book in the Barton Bible. In the second chapter it said:

"And so was he, great in power and influence among all the people. He arose on great wings as it were for all the people to see. They gazed in wonder and amazement." Who was this that was being written about? thought Callie. She read further and got more confused in doing so. She wondered if this being was an angel. In context, it certainly didn't appear to be Jesus – at least not the one she knew.

"Callie," interrupted Mom from the laundry room. "Can you come and get your clothes? You'll have to fold them yourself. I have to start dinner." That jolted her back to reality.

"Sure Mom," answered Callie. She wondered who folded clothes any more; she figured it was an old fashioned term for putting them away, and she did that in no time. She was wanting to go back and pursue her mystery-solving of the Book of Ambrose and his identity. She read further, deeper into the Book, several chapters in.

"It came to be that this Great Man revealed to only a few who he was and of what origin. He had no family and was as a sojourner in the land. He was befriended by man, but known by few. His home known to none, except the God over all. But the Great Man had prophecies to bring, and he was very wise and good. He traversed the region of that time, speaking to whoever would listen and helping those in need. He traveled alone except for the occasional time he was accompanied by companions from a far off country, a land of desert. His notoriety spread near and far.

Wow, thought Callie, this is a lot to wrap my head around. There still was no indication who this mystery man was. That night after dinner she thought she might delve in again and read further. There might be a clue to who she was reading about.

She would skip going on the computer and just go back to the Book of Ambrose. She read until she could read no further. Her mind was jumbled with questions. Should she write them down and ask just Mrs. Samuels? Maybe it would be easier. Still, if she did that, then it would be hard to launch her point of view like she had planned. She decided to let the matter rest till morning. She slept fitfully and even had a nightmare, something that hadn't happened in years. In her dream, she had conjured up an identity of this "Great Man", only he wasn't so great in her dream. For sure she couldn't tell Mom and Dad, or anyone else for that matter – not until she herself had solved the mystery of who he was.

*****

It wasn't until she ran into Mrs. Samuels, almost literally, in the grocery store that she was desperate enough at that point to ask the older woman about the identity of the man in the Alvin Barton Bible that she'd been reading about.

"Callie, I'm so glad we ran into each other, well, I don't mean *that* kind of running into each other," she laughed. "It just so happens we are going to be having a study on Ambrose this Saturday before our service. I'd love for you to come and I think it will answer all your questions."

"What time?" asked Callie.

"It will be at nine o'clock in the morning. You're welcome to stay for our service if you'd like."

"I'll see if I can go. I have a meeting of the Heaven Club that afternoon," replied Callie.

"Oh, how sweet," remarked Mrs. Samuels. *Sweet?* thought Callie. That was an odd way to put it.

"Well, I'll prob'ly see you then on Saturday. Bye," said Callie as she hurried to the checkout with the few groceries Mom had asked for. Thankfully, Mrs. Samuels hadn't critiqued the few items she had in her basket like last time she'd seen her there.

*****

Saturday arrived soon enough and Callie dressed in casual wear – nice slacks and a colorful spring sweater. She was surprised to note that the women and girls were all wearing dresses. She knew she stood out among the others. Oh well, she thought, they're prob'ly dressed up for their church service. She took a seat next to Mrs. Samuels who'd motioned for her to come to her. How could she refuse without causing a scene? So she went.

A tall elderly man approached the podium. He adjusted his glasses as he looked down at his notes. Then he looked up.

"Good morning, brethren. It's good to be with you on this fine Saturday. I hope all of you have been looking forward to this as much as I have. Lil and I have missed all of you since we were transferred to Crenshaw City. Let's begin with prayer, shall we?" Callie felt uncomfortable during the prayer. For one thing, she noticed that he didn't ask the prayer in Jesus' name at the end. She thought that was unusual since those prayers she'd heard were always asked in the name of Jesus. The other thing that made her uncomfortable was that she was in a room of veritable strangers, except for the few she'd met previously. "My name for those of you who don't know me," said the man at the podium, "is Jude Bartholomew – *Bishop* Jude Bartholomew."

"Today I will be speaking about a very revered man from within the pages of our own Alvin Barton Bible – Ambrose. Now many of you here already know his story, but some perhaps don't which is why I called for this Bible study. Ambrose existed from time immemorial, you might say. No one knows exactly what his origins were, except that he was of heavenly descent, created by God so to speak. He was sent to us during ancient as well as modern times – that being, say, two thousand years ago. His manifestations during each age of the Church have been sought fervently, and his messages are superb as you your-selves know if you've read the Book of Ambrose in your Bible. More than that, his prophecies were meant to enlighten and show us the way as we progress into more complicated times such as what we live in now." Callie tried to follow what the bishop was saying, but found herself becoming more confused by the minute. Her head was buzzing by the time the Bible study was over. Mrs. Samuels had used her own Alvin Barton Bible to show the verses that Bishop Bartholomew had referenced. Still, it made no sense to Callie at all.

"Well dear, I hope that answers your questions about our beloved Ambrose," said Mrs. Samuels when the Bible study was over.

"I really need to get going. Good bye, Mrs. Samuels," said Callie as she rushed to the door. She felt like she was ready to throw up. Maybe it was just the stuffiness of the room, she didn't know. But fresh air sounded really good. Once outside, she felt a little better. Her head cleared a bit and she could finally begin to think again. She practically ran home. Mom and Dad weren't home but Mom had left a note saying that she and Dad had gone to look for a big screen TV at one of the big box stores in neighboring Hunter Falls. She was just as glad they were gone since she really didn't want to talk to anyone, at least not yet. She had to make sense of what she'd heard at the Bible study.

Using logic, she knew a couple things for sure. One was that she'd never heard of the Book of Ambrose, let alone the Alvin Barton Bible. The second was everyone *she* knew used other versions of the Bible, but not that one. The third thing was that being around those people gave her the creeps. Maybe they were nice people otherwise but she just didn't fit in, nor did she want to. She resolved to avoid situations like that at all costs. She couldn't do much about running into Mrs. Samuels at the store or something, but she was going to make a concerted effort to keep her distance from them. Life had been going just fine before Mrs. Samuels had knocked on her front door. Before she did, though, she would take one last look at the Bible Mrs. Samuels had given her. Then she would stow it away in the garage somewhere and, hopefully, forget where she put it.

She examined the four gospels. Everything was in order. It read pretty much like her Bible did only without thee and thou and other words like it as in her King James Bible. The other books of the Bible seemed to be in order as well, at least in the New Testament. She did find in the Book of Genesis, several chapters in, a reference to Ambrose almost as if he were an angel. A verse caught her eye that she wouldn't soon forget:

And this Ambrose, a Sojourner from eternity, was worthy of the people's worship and they all paid him homage by building an altar and worshipped before it." What was *that* all about? She checked her Bible to see if that verse was in it and couldn't find it. She didn't remember ever reading it before. A couple years ago she'd read her Bible all the way through and there was no reference to anyone like that. Well, that was that, it's settled, she thought. No more of those people *or* their Bible.

CHAPTER FOURTEEN

The first of May dawned bright and Callie realized that the school year would soon be over. Summer vacation was just days away. It would be time to pick up a part- time summer job if she could find one and, of course, opportunity to spend more time with Sarah Jo as well as with Wendy and Laura. She'd hoped they could all get together like they did last summer. It was always fun when they were together. Of course, by now, Laura was maybe going steady, something she herself never planned to do. She felt that a sense of ownership over another individual was too limiting, too constricting, at a time when freedom to be who she was, was so important. Sarah Jo had told her about a friend, Macy, who went to public school in Addison where the Fosters used to live. Sarah Jo said she was very good looking and there were always guys after her, but Macy had a bad home life. Her father was very temperamental and did not spend much time with her. According to Sarah Jo, Macy had this need to have a guy around at all times, and the adoration of boys in general worked for her too. One boy in particular wanted to brand her as his own and he gave her his class ring. That led to jealousy on the part of other boys and one in particular. One day after school Macy's steady boyfriend and her other admirer met in the woods behind the school. Her boyfriend had acquired a knife that he'd planted a few days earlier when he knew he was going to have it out with the other boy. It turned out that in the foray, the admirer was very badly hurt and even lost the vision in one eye, not to mention acquired a scar on his face that was the calling card of a very sharp knife. No, Callie definitely didn't want to go steady.

It wasn't often that Callie went out on a school day, but today she wanted to surprise her parents with dinner. She knew Mom had not planned anything and it was her chance to do something nice for them. Like her grandma had always told her, "It's not the big things you do that count, it's the little things." She'd heard Mom say it more than once too, so she knew it was passed down through the generations. The question was, what to fix? She didn't want anything too fancy since she wasn't that good a cook herself. Something easy, yet yummy. Maybe beef stroganoff. She read the online recipe and found she had all the ingredients except one – sour cream. That could be easily remedied with a quick trip to Phil's Supermarket. It was such a beautiful day, Callie decided to walk; she could even count it as Phy Ed. She grabbed her coin purse and her cell phone and headed out the door.

Callie made a beeline to Dairy and found the sour cream. Maybe she'd also get an angel food cake and strawberries for dessert. Better pick up some whipping cream while she was still in the dairy aisle.

"Well, hello there, dear," a familiar voice came from behind her when she was in the produce department getting the strawberries. "Looks like *someone's* in for a treat."

"Uh yeh, I'm in charge of dinner tonight," said Callie who almost felt like she'd been caught stealing.

"Really?" said Mrs. Samuels. "I hate to be nosy, but what's on the menu?" Callie really didn't want to tell her but ended up blurting it out.

"Beef stroganoff."

"Well, how nice," said Mrs. Samuels in an odd tone of voice. "There are some great beef substitutes, but you won't find them here. There's a health food store over on Grand Avenue – they have everything."

"Uh, we like beef," said Callie almost apologetically.

"Have you had more time to read the Bible I gave you?" asked Mrs. Samuels, changing the subject.

"Well, not really. I've been busy with school."

"I see. Is this your Home Ec assignment?" asked Mrs. Samuels with a touch of sarcasm in her voice. Callie wasn't expecting that. "No matter," she continued. "I did want to talk to you about something though – something very important."

"Like what?" replied Callie. Mrs. Samuels nudged her to the side. "Well, you know a lot more about spiritual things now than before you met me. Do you realize God is going to hold you responsible for that?"

"I – I don't understand," stammered Callie.

"You know too much – plain and simple," declared Mrs. Samuels. "God is going to hold you accountable for what you know."

"Like *what?*" asked an incredulous Callie.

"Well, the Book of Ambrose, for starters," said Mrs. Samuels, lowering her voice. "You will need to make a commitment to this knowledge."

"I don't know what you're talking about, and I need to get going," said Callie, panicking.

"The important thing is that *God* knows. You can run away from me, but you can't run away from God." Callie dropped her grocery items down right in the middle of the strawberry display and rushed out the door of the supermarket. Her heart was pounding in her chest.

*****

"Callie, you're so quiet tonight. Is something wrong?" asked Mom at dinner. It turned out that Mrs. Morris ended up making dinner – fajitas.

"I just have a lot on my mind; end of the school year, you know," answered Callie, stretching the truth just a bit.

"Hey, girls, where do you want to go on vacation this year?" asked Dad, taking his cue from Callie's comment. "North, south, east or west – or any point between?"

"I guess it *isn't* too early to begin planning for vacation," said Mom, as she dabbed her mouth with a corner of her napkin.

"Once it gets warmer, it seems the days go quickly and we're all so busy," said Dad. "So it's a good time to be thinking about this. What do you think, Callie?"

"I don't know. Whatever anyone else wants is okay with me."

"I knew something wasn't right, Callie. What's bothering you?" asked Mom. "Last year you would've been jumping up and down with excitement."

"I'm older now," replied Callie.

"Well, being older doesn't necessarily mean you have to forgo enjoying life," said Mom as she passed the salsa over to her husband.

"I hope not!" added Dad. "I'm looking forward to getting away from it all."

"I guess no one has any ideas," Mom sighed.

"We could always go to Florida again," suggested Dad. "I know that Ted and June would roll out the red carpet – all the way to the beach!" Her parents laughed but Callie failed to see the humor in that or anything else at this point.

"Well, we have time yet," said Mom, "But now would be a good time to start thinking about it."

The thing was, Callie couldn't think of anything but what Mrs. Samuels had told her in the grocery store. *God is going to hold you accountable for what you know.* Those words were etched into her mind – and conscience. She *did* know about the Book of Ambrose, that was true. But she didn't know enough to make a commitment or maybe it was just that she knew *about* the Book of Ambrose. What kind of commitment was Mrs. Samuels talking about? She pondered these questions until finally she made up her mind to read the Book of Ambrose. Somehow she'd get through it even if she had no clue what it was talking about.

The best she could figure was that he was a mysterious being from somewhere. Callie decided to read it when her parents were at work the next day. She was pretty much where she needed to be with her school work so she was okay there.

The next morning after Mom and Dad had left and the house was quiet, she took the Alvin Barton Bible into the living room and arranged herself in Dad's comfy rocker recliner and began to read the Book of Ambrose. Her plan was to read it all the way through in one sitting – if she didn't fall asleep. It had thirteen chapters to it and a couple of them were quite long. It wasn't easy reading. The beginning was rather poetic, but as the chapters dragged on they became more cumbersome and whatever message contained within, more cryptic. It was like reading a mystery only without a destination, a conclusion.

Words were swirling around in her head: devastation, despair, anguish. Was this what was talked about in certain books of the Bible she used? And how did Ambrose fit in with all of this? She plodded onward in her reading. Finally, she came to the last couple of chapters. It seemed, from what she could tell so far, that this Ambrose was going to supersede all powers and win victory over all the earth. That was confusing. Wasn't that the job of Jesus?

When she finally read the very last chapter of the Book of Ambrose, she was thoroughly confused. It made no sense to her at all. The only thing she concluded was that Ambrose was victorious in the end. That just didn't square with what Jesus did on Calvary's cross because *He* was the only one who won victory by what He did.

Callie had planned to call Sarah Jo and ask her about the Alvin Barton Bible she'd been given, but then changed her mind. It might make her look dumb and Sarah Jo might ask how she got herself into this mess. No, Callie determined she'd keep researching this until she got to the bottom of it. But on this particular day she needed to go to the office supply store and get a new cartridge for her printer. The store was only a few blocks away so she decided to get some exercise and walk over. School was over for the day anyhow so she didn't feel uncomfortable being out like she would if public school was still in session. There was a newer office supply store on the other side of town but Mr. Cady had been here as far back as she could remember. Many people thought the newer store would drive him out of business, but apparently not. He was here to stay, he'd declared.

"Hi young lady," greeted Mr. Cady from behind the cash register. "Need some help?" Callie was sure that the reason he was still in business was because of his friendly smile and good service.

"No, not right now, Mr. Cady," she answered. "Just looking for an ink cartridge for my printer."

"Okay, well you know where they are." As she checked out the display, she heard the old-fashioned bell high up on the door jingle again as it had when *she'd* entered.

"Uhh.. hi," came the deep male voice. Callie looked up. That face was familiar. "Aren't you the girl who spoke to our church group about home school?"

"Yes, that was me." She found her cartridge.

"You probably don't remember me but I'm Austin. I asked you a question there."

"Oh yeh. I remember you now. You asked about the pros and cons of home school, didn't you?"

"Yep."

"Do you think you'll want to do home school?" asked Callie.

"Well, I don't know. I've been in regular school from the start. It's worked okay for me so far."

"Great," said Callie. "Whatever works, as they say."

"I just came in to get some printer paper. I go through that like water," he chuckled.

"I spose you do, like with turning in papers and stuff."

"Right," confirmed Austin.

"Not so much with home school and online studies," said Callie.

"Hey, if you don't have to go right back home, do you wanna go to Snackers for a soda or something?" Callie noticed how considerably his face had reddened as he asked.

"Sure, I guess so," she answered. She didn't have to be home right away, so why not? They paid for their items and left the store. Snackers was only a block down from there. There was an awkward silence between them and then they both spoke in unison about the weather they were having. Both laughed.

Finally seated at their table each with a soda, Callie started the conversation.

"So, you must know Mrs. Samuels pretty well."

"Yep, she's what I suppose you'd call a pillar in the church – always there, if you know what I mean," said Austin. Callie nodded. It almost seemed like this shy guy had something on his mind, but she wasn't going to pry.

"So, you've been a member of that church all your life then." She spoke it as if it were a fact and it turned out that it was.

"Yep, as far back as I can remember."

"Your church seems interesting, but I didn't even know where it was until I spoke that day," said Callie.

"Well, we don't shout it from the rooftops. We kinda figure people will find it if God wants them to. He's the one who finds the members, I guess you'd say," said Austin.

"*Really?!* I guess that's one way to bring in members. But other people in their own churches would figure that they're in their church cuz God brought them there too."

"Well, *all* churches can't be right, can they?" asked Austin, striving to lend credence to his comments.

"I spose not, but it's not so much what you do that identifies you as a Christian, but what you believe," declared Callie. "At least that's what I've always thought. The works will follow."

"Have you been a Christian all your life?" asked Austin.

"Well, I've gone to the same church since I was born, but I didn't accept Jesus until I was twelve."

"What do you mean by 'accept Jesus' exactly?" asked Austin as he finished his soda. "Do you want a refill?"

"No, not yet," answered Callie. Austin excused himself and brought his refill back.

"So, you were saying...?" he said as he sat down.

"Well, I'm just saying that the gospel message tells us we need to acknowledge we're a sinner and then accept what Jesus did for us on the cross. Why? What did you think I meant?" asked Callie. She took a sip of her soda.

"Well... we have Ambrose, as in the Book of Ambrose."

"Yes, I know. I was at that Bible study a few weeks ago. What about him – Ambrose, I mean?" asked Callie. Maybe she would finally get the answers to her questions – research over.

"He's very important," said Austin with obvious reverence and awe.

"How so?" pressed Callie. Austin glanced down at his watch.

"Look, I've gotta go. My mother's going to wonder why it took so long to get the printer paper."

"Wait," said Callie. "Can't you spare a few more minutes?" She wanted an answer to her question. But it was not to be.

"Sorry," apologized Austin as his chair scraped against the vinyl flooring. "Gotta get going."

After her shock wore off, Callie hatched a plan that she hoped might bring Austin back at least into her universe. She was going to invite him to one of their teen Bible studies. For her, that was pretty gutsy seeing as how she wasn't the most courageous person. It would mean contacting Mrs. Samuels to either get Austin's number or for Mrs. Samuels to relay the invitation to him herself.

She figured the latter might work best. She'd wait until tomorrow to execute this latest plan on her quest to find out just who Ambrose was.

Callie felt bad that she hadn't kept in touch more with the girls. She was sure Wendy and Laura had interesting things to tell her, but they'd have to wait. Sarah Jo too. The next day was Friday and Callie wasted no time in calling Mrs. Samuels. She had to hurry and do it or she might chicken out. This was setting a very bad precedent, but she had to do it. Even so, her efforts might be in vain. She punched in the number.

"Hello, dear. I saw your number on my caller ID."

"Oh hi, Mrs. Samuels," said Callie, trying to sound casual.

"How are you doing, dear?" asked the pleasant sounding voice.

"I'm fine, thanks."

"What can I do for you?" asked Mrs. Samuels.

"Well uh, I kind of have a favor to ask of you. I mean if it isn't too much trouble."

"What would that be? I'll help if I can. You've surely helped me."

"Well, I was thinking back to when I told your group about home schooling?" she posed it as a question.

"Yes," confirmed Mrs. Samuels.

"Well, a group of us teens are holding a Bible study at my place next Thursday night at seven o'clock. I had thought about that one boy in your group who'd asked that excellent question about the pros and cons of home school."

"Oh you mean Austin Reynolds?"

"Yes, I guess so," answered Callie, trying to sound vague.

"So, what about him?" asked Mrs. Samuels.

"Well, it seems he asks good questions and might have something to contribute to our Bible study."

"I can see where you'd get that from," commented Mrs. Samuels. "So, what would you like *me* to do – the favor, that is?"

"Well, I would appreciate it if you could ask if he'd like to go. I don't call boys so it would be great if you could let him know. There will be other guys there his age and dress is casual." Wow! Where did she summon the courage to speak like that – especially to Mrs. Samuels?

"I suppose I could speak to him at services this week. I know your address, but what was the time again?"

"Seven o'clock." answered Callie.

As Thursday approached, Callie wondered if maybe Mrs. Samuels had thought better of the favor she'd asked – or maybe she even forgot to ask Austin. It was with no small amount of trepidation that Callie planned the Bible study. For one thing, she did *not* want to host it on this particular night, so even though it would be held at her house, she asked Donnie Maxwell if he'd do the honors. If Austin actually showed up, he might feel more comfortable with a guy conducting it. Mom said she'd be there, just as Mrs. Foster had been for the Bible study at Sarah Jo's. Even Dad said he'd be around. So, with all the snacks taken care of, Callie could reasonably expect it to be a good night. She even provided some whole grain bars because of what Mrs. Samuels had said in the grocery store when Olivia had chosen the neon-colored cereal. She figured that their church's beliefs didn't include eating foods like that but, rather, those that were more natural.

After clearing off the dinner dishes and putting them in the dishwasher, Callie ran a comb through her hair but decided to pass on the lipstick. Once again, she felt it might be offensive to Austin and she didn't want to do that, sort of like it said in the Bible about eating meat in the presence of a vegetarian.

One by one, the teens arrived. No Austin. Callie had a feeling that it was just too much to expect. Donnie started the Bible study with prayer. As the last amen was spoken, there was a knock on the door. Callie hurried to answer it in hopes that Austin had been able to make it. She had already told the group about him attending, and asked that they didn't pepper him with questions. She opened the door.

"Oh hi, Austin," greeted Callie. "Glad you could make it. Come on in."

"Hi," said Austin shyly. Callie knew this must be hard for him.

"Just grab a seat anywhere. There's a chair next to where I'm sitting, if you want it. Hey everyone, this is Austin Reynolds." There were various greetings from those in the room.

"I'm Callie's mom – Mrs. Morris," Callie's mother introduced herself. "Make yourself comfortable, Austin." Austin decided to sit next to Callie. Donnie proceeded with the Bible study.

"So, what topic do you want to discuss tonight?" he asked as he looked around the room. "Yes Lydia," he acknowledged her raised hand.

"I think we should talk about the different rites and rituals in the different churches," she answered.

"Naw," said Riley Woodboro. "Who wants to know *that* stuff? Different churches do different things. They all do it with the intention of honoring God."

"Well, I think it would be interesting," replied Lydia.

"It might be," said Donnie, "but there are topics that might be *more* interesting."

"Why don't we discuss the cross?" asked Callie. She didn't want to waste time with trying to figure out a topic.

"Good call, Cal," said Donnie. "How about this? Why don't we each explain what the cross means to us?" Everyone nodded in agreement.

Callie noticed that Austin looked perplexed; sort of like he didn't know whether to nod or not.

"I'll start," said LeAnn with her hand raised.

"Go ahead, LeAnn," said Donnie.

"Well, years ago for my birthday I got a necklace that had a cross on it. My aunt had given it to me. I was pretty young at the time and I just thought it was something sorta pretty; I mean it was gold and all – maybe not real gold, but it was pretty. In the middle of it there was a ruby, prob'ly not a real one though. One day I was visiting my aunt. My mother had told me to wear it over there since that would show my appreciation for it, so I did. When my aunt saw it she said, 'Oh good, you're wearing the cross I gave you. Do you know what it stands for?' I told her no, because no one had explained it to me. She told me what it meant, and all about Jesus and what He did."

"So, what did you do then?" asked Sarah Jo.

"She asked me if I'd like to pray and ask Jesus into my life," answered LeAnn. "So I did, but it wasn't till a few years later that I really under-stood why I needed His sacrifice." That was after I started going to church with Aunt Ginny. Mother and Daddy said I could."

"Cool," said Riley. The others added their own words of approval – except for Austin who had seemed to pull into his own shell.

One by one each gave their testimony of the cross, except Austin, and ended with Callie. She made her comments brief since she didn't want to burden Austin with too much information – even if it was the good kind. Nor did she want Austin to feel uncomfortable by speaking at this Bible study. He looked like didn't want to be called on, just by what Callie noticed with his body language.

"Who's ready for refreshments?" asked Callie. "They're in on the dining room table there. Help yourself." Austin got up with the rest and, much to Callie's delight, he chose a granola bar as did some of the others. Each of the teens left – all except Austin.

"Hey Austin, before you leave, can I ask you something?" Callie had hoped to find out more about this Ambrose before Austin got away from her. She'd much rather find out from him than Mrs. Samuels; and her own research was netting nothing. It seemed that Ambrose was the world's best kept secret.

"Uh, sure, what is it?"

"Well, remember when we were talking about the Book of Ambrose when we were at Snackers? I need to know who he is." Austin's countenance changed visibly. He became agitated and he frowned.

"It's not for us to know," he mumbled.

"You mean *you* don't even know who he is?" asked Callie incredulously.

"We're not told – only what the Book of Ambrose reveals about him."

"Who wrote the Book of Ambrose – Ambrose himself?" Austin started toward the door.

"That's what we're told," he answered.

"Wait," said Callie. "Then who is Jesus Christ in your Bible?"

"He was a teacher and prophet as well as a very good man," replied Austin.

"But that's all?" asked Callie.

"Pretty much. I guess people called him a healer and it appears he did have sorta magical powers. It doesn't really matter since he did good deeds for the people one way or the other," said Austin, then his tone of voice changed. "Hey look, I gotta get going. I told my mother I'd be home before nine."

"Do you need a ride or something? My dad could drive you home," said Callie.

"No! I mean no thanks. It's not that far to walk. It'll take me about twenty minutes if I leave now," said Austin. Callie believed it. With his long legs, he'd make pretty good time.

"Okay, bye. Thanks for coming tonight," called Callie to the lanky boy who had disappeared into the night. He's almost as mysterious as Ambrose, thought Callie. Oh well...

CHAPTER FIFTEEN

Callie was glad that school was over for another year! It wasn't that she disliked school, just that she was glad to be out from under the pressure. She couldn't even imagine what public school was like, although they offered certain things that would've been nice to get involved in such as social activities. Now that summer was approaching, though, she'd make up for lost time in that department. Callie looked forward to getting together with Sarah Jo and Wendy and Laura. They always had fun at their sleepovers. After all, that's how the Heaven Club got started.

Callie still puzzled over Ambrose, and Austin's unusual attitude toward the subject. No matter how badly she wanted to solve *that* mystery, she wasn't about to ask Mrs. Samuels anything about it. It would just have to stay unsolved.

One afternoon a few weeks after the last teen Bible study that Austin had attended, there was a knock at the door. Callie peered out the window to the side of the door but she couldn't see who it was, just a figure near the door.

"Who is it?" she asked, not willing to let anyone in. Still, it could be a delivery person who needed her signature. Every so often that happened.

"It's me – Austin."

"Austin?" She slowly opened the door, but not far enough so that he could enter.

"Uh yeh, it's me. I wonder if we could talk for a few minutes."

"I'm not allowed to let anyone in when I'm here alone – house rules, you know." He nodded. "But I suppose we could go out on the deck."

"Sure, that'd be fine," he answered. What in the world could *he* want? thought Callie as she went to the back door. The deck was nicely warmed in the late spring sunshine.

"Have a seat," she offered.

"Thanks," he replied shyly as he sat down on a bench on the perimeter of the deck. Callie found a chair with cushions and sat down.

"So, what's on your mind?" she asked. Austin looked down at his hands.

"I figured I was kind of rude after the Bible study when you asked me that question."

"Oh, you mean about Ambrose?" she asked.

"Uh... yeh."

"Well, I guess I just don't understand what the big mystery is all about," she said.

"You wouldn't understand unless you were one of us," said Austin who looked like he was in physical pain by just even explaining this to Callie.

"One of us?" she repeated.

"Someone in our church," he clarified.

"Well, the Gospel message is easily understood; even a child can make sense of it," commented Callie.

"Our message comes from Ambrose," Austin said. "It's what we live by."

"Yes, but who *is* Ambrose?"

"He is the one who will save this world, but that time hasn't come yet. At least that's what we're taught."

"Jesus Christ already *did* that," said Callie.

"You've got to be kidding! With the shape this world's in?"

"He sacrificed Himself for this world. Haven't you ever read John 3:16?" asked Callie as she began to see how off-the-wall Austin's beliefs were. "It says: 'For God so loved the world that He gave His only begotten Son, that whoever believes in Him should not perish but have everlasting life.'"

"Well, I'm sure I have, but in what context?"

"Context? There *is* only one context and it has to do with us sinners," declared Callie. "Only that."

"What about Ambrose? It's just like you're totally leaving him out," said Austin, sounding a bit annoyed.

"What *about* Ambrose?" Callie shot back. She wanted to know. "He's not Jesus."

"Of course not," said Austin emphatically. "Jesus was a good man and a prophet."

"You mean to tell me that you don't believe that Jesus Christ wasn't – isn't – divine; that He isn't God?"

"What are you talking about?" asked Austin, who looked bewildered. "Look, I didn't come over to debate who Jesus Christ was – I already know! I came for a different reason." Callie was totally lost at that point.

"*Huh?*"

"Yeah, there's something else I wanted to talk with you about, but maybe now isn't a good time."

"It's as good a time as any," replied Callie.

"Look, along with an apology for the other night, I just want to say that you and I are very different. I mean our beliefs are nowhere on the same page or even book; maybe not even in the same library."

"Well, I think I figured that out," said Callie with just a hint of sarcasm in her voice. Austin didn't pick up on it.

"I know our church's beliefs must seem strange to you, plus we have a lot of rules that we have to follow."

"You know," said Callie. "I really don't know enough about your church to say one way or the other, but I'll put it this way: your church has got the most important part wrong."

"Huh? How do you figure?"

"If you really want to know, I'll tell you, but I don't see much good coming from arguing about our different beliefs," said Callie. The back door swung open.

"Well hello, you two," greeted Mom. "I didn't see you in the house, Callie, so I thought I'd check back here. I'm going to start dinner pretty soon. Maybe you can help me in about a half hour."

"Sure Mom."

"Nice seeing you again, Mrs. Morris," said Austin.

"Likewise, Austin," she replied, then closed the door.

"Look, I don't want to start anything here," said Austin in a subdued voice. I just wanted to talk about something with you and the previous subject wasn't it."

"Well, exactly *what* then?" asked Callie.

"Well, things haven't been easy for me, going to public school and all," confessed Austin. "Sure, I'm used to it, but it doesn't mean I'm having a great time."

"What's the problem?" asked Callie.

"Well, like I said, we have a lot of rules that we follow in our church."

"*And ... ?*" asked Callie.

"Well, I kinda like sports – like basketball," said Austin.

"Sooooo...?"

"Our church doesn't allow it. Not so much because it's sports, but mostly because of the uniforms when they play."

"*What?*" You mean the shorts and tops the guys wear?"

"Yep! Our church thinks they're improper, that they show too much, uh, skin."

"Well, how else can you play decent?" asked Callie. "What do they expect you to wear – sweats?"

"I guess so. I never got that far in the discussion."

"Wow!" Callie didn't know what to say. She'd never heard of anything like that before.

"Hey, don't tell anyone I told you this. You're the first person I've mentioned it to."

"Uh, sure," Callie promised. "I won't."

"I think I'd better go now. It's getting late. Like I said, it takes about twenty minutes to get home from here."

"Thanks for sharing this with me, Austin," said Callie. "I know it wasn't easy to do that."

"Right," he answered, confirming her hunch. "Talk to you later."

*****

Her discussion with Austin lingered with her throughout the night. She was thankful at dinner that she needed to pay attention to the table conversation or her parents would become suspicious; it gave her a break from her thoughts that were speeding like a runaway train. How could Austin not know the truth about Jesus Christ? What kind of a church would teach someone whose identity was a total mystery was going to save the world? The whole thing seemed creepy to her. Then add to that the idea of not being able to play basketball because Austin wasn't allowed to wear a conventional uniform for it – that put the frosting on the cake, as Mom would put it. It just made no sense. She immediately felt sorry for Austin. He was tall and seemed suited to basketball. Callie imagined him being able to sink the final – and decisive – basket at a game. Heady stuff! But something he probably wouldn't get to experience. That was too bad since that was one of the perks of public school, in her opinion.

Callie was getting together with the Addison girls at a sleepover at Sarah Jo's, but that wasn't for about another month. After the girl talk, they often delved into deeper subjects, especially spiritual ones. She didn't know yet if she wanted to bring up Mrs. Samuels and her Future Life Fellowship or even the Alvin Barton Bible and Ambrose. It just seemed that it might invite their judgment upon her. Not that they'd be malicious, but words from friends could be hurtful sometimes. She could just hear Sarah Jo scolding her: "How did you get mixed up with these people?" or "You're too trusting, Cal." Well, what could she have done when Mrs. Samuels came to her door with a little girl that had to use the bathroom? Callie relived the drama over and over in her mind.

Sunday – and church – was a welcome change to the long week.

Plus it distanced her from Austin's and her weird conversation. Pastor Martin was all smiles during his sermon.

"Today is a very good day," he proclaimed, "for someone, somewhere. There's somebody who has come to know their need for Jesus Christ in their life and has accepted Him as their Saviour. He has come to abide within that person who has been set free from their sins. How can we be so blessed, those of us who know Him in this way? How could something so horrid for Him, be such a wonderful blessing for *us*? His suffering, death, burial and resurrection was done for us. Can we appreciate that type of love?"

Callie could. But she knew that it was easy to take for granted what Jesus had done on the cross for mankind. She herself needed to get in touch with what He'd done for her. Her thoughts shifted to Austin. What about him? Where was his hope? Locked up in the person of a mysterious being who supposedly will save the world. Who lived within him? Callie tried to ignore the chill she felt. She knew she couldn't let him labor under the delusion that some being named Ambrose had won salvation for him, which she knew wasn't true. Her mind ruminated on this conundrum.

"And so, my brothers and sisters in the Lord, we must be on fire with love and dedication to serve and help those less fortunate than we are. Find someone who needs the Good Word – the Gospel message – and minister to him or her. Make it a good day for that person." Those words swirled around in her mind. This could be her "project" for the Heaven Club. She'd been working with Sarah Jo helping senior citizens that had need, but this would be something more specific.

Project Austin! Of course, she couldn't tell the others about it – at least not yet.

*****

There was another teen Bible study and, wonder of wonders, Austin attended. He'd called Callie – probably got her number through Mrs. Samuels – and found out when and where. Callie volunteered to hold it at her house again so that it would be easier on Austin, although she didn't tell the others that. She just volunteered, and they accepted.

So, once again, Austin ended up at her door on the night of the Bible study. This time he came earlier. That was good, thought Callie; he'd feel more a part of the group that way. This time she conducted the study, since she hadn't last time. She had more courage now after hearing Pastor Martin's sermon and since she determined she would be working on Project Austin. She chose a subject that would be of interest to all, but nothing too heavy duty: What commandment of the ten commandments do you feel is most needed in these times? A variety of answers followed, each with its own merits.

"Well," said Callie at the end of the discussion, "maybe this is why God gave us ten and not just one." The teens nodded. All had gone well at this Bible study. She noted that Austin had chosen the first of the ten commandments: I *am* the Lord your God, who brought you out of the land of Egypt, out of the house of bondage. You shall have no other gods before Me.

It seemed ironic that Austin should pick that one since Ambrose certainly could not make that claim. She hadn't noticed any reference of that sort in the Book of Ambrose. When Austin had been asked why he had chosen that particular commandment, he'd suddenly become self-conscious and mumbled something about it being the most important commandment. Riley had questioned it, and Austin replied tersely that the commandments wouldn't have any meaning without God.

Callie said good bye to her friends and, once again, Austin was the only one who remained.

"I'm glad you came tonight, Austin," said Callie.

"Me too. I like everybody who was here."

"So," ventured Callie, "is this pretty much what they teach at your church?"

"I don't know everything your church teaches," replied Austin as he cleared his throat. "We're taught that a lot of churches are wrong."

"Wrong about what exactly?"

"Well, you know, about other churches' teachings. I mean they have the wrong Bible for starters," he answered. That shocked Callie, but she pressed on.

"Why? Because they don't have the Book of Ambrose?"

"For starters, yes," said Austin. "You can't just leave him out of something as important as the Bible."

Yes, you can, thought Callie, if he was never in there to begin with.

"Well, I've never seen his name written or mentioned in the Bible or anywhere else, for that matter," said Callie. She didn't say it in an accusing tone of voice; she didn't want to argue. She simply said it because it was true.

"You make my point," declared Austin. "Why do you think this world is in so much turmoil?" Callie was taken aback.

"Uh... because of human beings without the Holy Spirit living within them?"

"Are you *serious?*" They're sometimes the *cause* of problems," he argued.

"Well, not the ones I know. They are very dedicated to the Lord and serving Him. Of course there are nominal Christians – those who sit in church for an hour a week but forget about God the rest of the time. You prob'ly have a few of those in *your* church too."

"Touché," conceded Austin. "Well, I better get going."

"Thanks again for joining us tonight," said Callie. That went well, thought Callie as she shut the door. Score one for Project Austin!

CHAPTER SIXTEEN

It wasn't till after her sleepover with Wendy and Laura at Sarah Jo's that she had the opportunity to talk to Austin again. But by then she was fired up from iron sharpening iron as Dad put it, with her friends. Yes, they had talked about hair and make-up and even the latest fashions, but they did get around to talking about spiritual things and it was an eye-opener for Callie. Her three friends had grown by leaps and bounds spiritually, so much so that she wondered if she was bringing up the rear in that department.

Wendy told her friends that she and Mrs. Elkins had actually talked about God in the context of Mrs. Elkins' husband's safety during service in the military. That was huge since Mrs. Elkins was a self-proclaimed atheist; well, sort of. At least the name of God had been brought up, Wendy had pointed out to her friends who heartily agreed. As for Laura, no, she was not going with any guy and, yes, she'd tried to make inroads with Andy and Damian. Laura felt they were interested in her, but not in her message so she thought it might be quite hopeless since she wasn't interested in a relationship with either of them. So they all agreed they'd continue to pray about it.

As for Callie and Sarah Jo, they told of their involvement with the elderly. There were a few things that had happened that were both significant, and others that were kind of humorous. They shared both.

"For one thing," explained Sarah Jo, "These are people nearing the other end of life. It seems that they start getting serious about it at a certain point."

"Yes, but there are others who don't want to think about it," added

Callie. "One man asked me what plans I have for the future. I told him I hadn't made up my mind yet but that I knew God would direct me in that decision. Then he said, 'I didn't ask you what plans God had, I asked what *your* plans are.'" The girls laughed, but it was also sad because most people didn't understand how important God is to a Christian believer, thought Callie in retrospect.

Austin had called and asked to meet her in the park in the afternoon and she'd said yes. She didn't want to miss out on any opportunity to make progress with Project Austin.

*****

A gentle late May breeze seemed to be trying to coax the new leaves out on the trees. Although not in full leaf, it was refreshing to see a haze of green over the clusters of trees in the park. She found Austin leaning against the ladder to the slide in the middle of the park.

"Hi," Callie called out to the tall, lean boy. He turned around quickly.

"Oh hi, Callie. Guess I was deep in thought."

"Do I want to know about what?" asked Callie as she wondered if she was overstepping the bounds of their relationship.

"Just about life. Sometimes it's all so confusing," he confessed.

"Well, I have to admit there are times when things aren't always clear," agreed Callie. "But there's always an answer if a person looks for it."

"I spose, but it's not like a formula that works every time. Wanna sit on the swings?" Callie figured this would be a serious discussion since there would be no face-to-face conversation, at least to begin with.

"Sure," she sat on a swing next to Austin. "So, what's up?" He stared down at the ground for a few minutes.

"Ever wonder how high these things can go?" He lifted his feet off the ground and began pumping, propelling himself higher and higher.

"I don't think I *want* to know," said Callie, her voice cautionary. Austin took the cue and, using his feet as brakes, finally slowed to a stop.

"Here's the thing," said Austin. "All my life I've been a member of

FLF – Future Life Fellowship. I'm not complaining; my life has been mostly good. It's just that I wonder what I've been missing out on."

"Such as..." volunteered Callie.

"Well, like I told you about playing basketball. Do you know how many people have asked me why I don't go out for basketball?"

"Go on."

"Well, it's embarrassing – plus it hurts. Just a constant reminder about the fact that I can't."

"Do they know the reason?"

"Not exactly. I've made excuses," said Austin.

"Can I ask you a question?"

"Sure Callie – shoot."

"What do you wear in Phy Ed? I mean you can't wear your street clothes." Austin's face reddened.

"I sorta went and bought gym clothes on my own. I did odd jobs over the summer and accumulated some cash."

"Oh, so your parents didn't know anything about it then." It was more of a statement than a question.

"You got it!" said Austin.

"Wow..." said Callie, half aloud. "Just wow..."

"Now do you see what I mean?" asked Austin as he brushed a lady bug off his pant leg. Callie nodded, even though it was hard for her to put herself in his shoes. For a few minutes, neither said anything. Callie broke the silence.

"There's something that kinda concerns me more about your situation though."

"What's that?"

"Well, have you thought of the spiritual side of things?" she asked, looking in his direction.

"Callie, that's *all* I think about! I mean that's what this is all about. I think of kids in school who don't give their religion a second thought. I mean maybe they should but they don't – at least it doesn't seem that way. They're just kids going to school. They have lives outside the doors of their church, although in our church we think that's a lot what's wrong with kids today."

"Well, I don't belong to your church, yet you've come to me rather than to someone in your *own* church," said Callie.

"Right. Because they don't understand."

"And I do." Again she put it as a statement.

"Well, yeh, more than *they* do. How can they be objective?" asked Austin. For the first time, he looked in her direction. She could see the desperation in his eyes.

"I can see your point."

"I mean, look, time is passing by. I'll never have this opportunity again to play basketball in high school. I've tried to keep up with our church's rules and regulations, but my heart's not in it. How is it fair that I have to do all that stuff they tell us to do, but I can't ever have things the way I want them?"

"We all have things we don't want to do," said Callie who admired his openness in sharing what was a heavy burden for him.

"Sure, I know that, but have you ever wanted something so bad you could taste it and no matter what you did, it just wouldn't happen?" asked Austin.

"I think everyone has had that happen. I know I have. But then something even better comes my way," said Callie. It didn't help that some young kids, Callie guessed about ten or eleven, were shooting hoops in the adjacent basketball court. It was obvious they were having great fun.

"See, that's what I mean, Callie. Look at those guys. I bet one of them – or more – will go out for basketball in high school. No one will tell them they can't." Callie looked to see why she didn't hear the ball bouncing off the blacktop and got her answer. The ball was stuck in the net.

"Aw, the park people must've put up new nets this spring – too tight to let the basketball through," said Austin as he got up and walked over to the hoop. "Need some help?" The boys nodded. Austin jumped up and pushed the ball through the net.

"May I?" asked Austin. Again the boys nodded and Austin dribbled the ball, whipped around and dunked it hard into the net. He repeated the process several times until the ball slid through the net without hanging up in it. The boys looked on in awe.

"There, that should help." He ambled back to the swings as the boys resumed their play.

"I guess you're their hero now," said Callie.

"Guess so," mumbled Austin, smiling.

"You know in the Bible where it says we're to seek first the kingdom of God?"

"Sure Callie, our church tells us that all the time." replied Austin glumly.

"Well, I was going to tell you about something that concerns me more than your unfulfilled dream of playing basketball in school."

"Which would be what exactly?"

"I'm not sure how to put this, but when it comes to a saviour Jesus Christ is the only one I know," said Callie with deep conviction.

"As opposed to...?" challenged Austin.

"Let me put it this way, if I were to ask you who *your* saviour is, what would be your answer?" asked Callie. She stared at his profile, since he wouldn't look in her direction.

"Is this a trick question or something? I just wanted someone to talk to, someone I can trust."

"If you trust me, why won't you answer my question?" asked Callie. Flustered by Callie pressing him he blurted out his answer.

"I don't know! Ambrose? It can't be Christ. He was just a man – a very good one, as well as a prophet. Why are you asking me these things?"

"Because this is the heart and core of the gospel message. What do you think the gospel is about?" Callie persisted.

"I don't know – about Jesus, about Ambrose? Ambrose will do the saving," answered Austin.

"How do you know that, Austin?"

"It says so in the Book of Ambrose." Callie couldn't recall anything specific about Ambrose's salvation capabilities mentioned in his Book in the Alvin Barton Bible Mrs. Samuels had given her.

"Do you consider yourself a Christian?" asked Callie, knowing she was about at the end of Austin's patience.

"Of course I'm a Christian – why?" he answered.

"Because a Christian is a follower of Christ. You're a follower of Ambrose so you should technically be called an 'Ambrosian'."

"What?" asked Austin incredulously. He glared in her direction.

"Well, shouldn't you?" she asked. There was a heavy silence, save for the basketball bouncing and the young boys' voices as they played. All of a sudden Austin burst out laughing and then so did Callie. He didn't stop until he was gasping for air. It was like all this pent up frustration rolled out of him in the form of laughter.

She wiped a tear that had escaped her eye and was rolling down her cheek.

"'Ambrosian'" he repeated and began laughing again. "It just sounds so funny."

"Yes," agreed Callie. "Like you're from the planet Ambrosia." That brought another round of laughter. Suddenly Austin stopped laughing.

"I shouldn't be laughing. It doesn't show respect to the person and teachings of Ambrose," said Austin.

"I agree," Callie found herself saying. "That's why I think you should really find out who Ambrose is – then compare him to Jesus and what He did." Callie knew there was no comparison, but it might keep Austin's mind open to checking Ambrose out as well as to read the gospels in depth. What he said next shocked Callie.

"Will you help me with that?"

"Are you kidding me?" she answered. "Of course I will." His face reflected gratitude.

"Well, I'd better get going or my parents will wonder where I am. I'll call you soon." He got up and loped off into the distance. Project Austin was going better than she could've imagined.

CHAPTER SEVENTEEN

"Callie... phone," called Mom from the kitchen. Callie was in her bedroom and she thought she'd heard the phone ring, but wasn't sure. She was listening to music and rearranging her closet.

"Okay Mom," she answered. "I'll take it on the office phone." She wondered why the caller didn't just call on her cell phone. She picked up the heavy cordless – compared to her cell.

"Hi, Callie?" It was Austin.

"Yes, it's me." She heard the click of Mom hanging up the phone in the kitchen.

"You sound just like your mom."

"I do?"

"Yep. Hey, I wanted to ask you something," said Austin.

"I want to ask you something first. Why didn't you call my cell phone? Not that it matters – just wondering."

"Uhh... I couldn't get through." Callie pulled out her phone. She'd forgotten to charge it. Well, that would explain it. "It needs charging. Guess I forgot."

"No problem. There's always the good old landlines," said Austin.

"Okay, so what did you want to ask me?"

"Well uh, I was just wondering if you were having another teen Bible study."

"Let's see," answered Callie. "It looks like one's coming up here not this week, but the week after – on Thursday. You're welcome to come, you know. In fact, if you don't everyone will prob'ly wonder where you are."

"Really?" chuckled Austin. "I didn't know I was that important."

"Well, none of us are, and all of us are. Figure that one out," replied Callie with a chuckle also.

"Well, I'd like to know where everyone's meeting. Is it at your place again?" asked Austin.

"Nope, not this time. It will be held at Donnie Maxwell's place. He lives three blocks down from me on Orchard Street, 2313 to be exact."

"Same time?"

"Yep, seven o'clock, on Thursday like I mentioned," said Callie.

After she hung up, Callie had what she felt was a brilliant idea. Why not have the theme of the study center on the person of Jesus. That would certainly fit in nicely with Project Austin. That is, if Donnie would go along with it. Technically, it was his call since the Bible study was being held at his house. And who knows how Austin would react. He might think it was a set-up. Oh well, thought Callie, too bad. God comes first. He needed to know who Jesus is.

Callie talked to Donnie at church that week about delving into having Jesus as the topic of the study.

"I already had a subject picked out, Cal," said Donnie. "But gee, if it's that important to you, we can talk about Him."

"Well, I just think people need to be reminded of who He is since He plays such an important role in all of our lives."

People were hurrying in to take their seats, but Callie didn't care. This was important.

"Can't argue about that. Then Jesus it is. I'll make sure He's the topic." Now, thought Callie, if only Austin shows up as promised.

*****

Callie was to learn something about her new friend – or maybe about the principles of his church. When they give their word, they keep it. It was true of Mrs. Samuels and it was also true of Austin.

The usual group of teens, save Austin, had gathered at the Maxwell home. It was just before seven that Thursday evening. A knock brought

Callie to the front door. She knew it would be Austin, and Donnie was in the kitchen anyway.

"Hey Callie," said Austin. "You live here too?" They shared a laugh.

"No, just playing host till Donnie gets back," said Callie. "He's in the other room. C'mon in." Soon everyone had seated themselves and Donnie took over.

"Glad everyone could make it tonight," he said as he looked in Austin's direction. Callie wasn't sure if Austin caught that, but it didn't matter. The main thing was, he was here. "Okay, let's get started here with a short prayer. Anyone want to do the honors?"

"I will," volunteered Sarah Jo. After finishing, Donnie began the study.

"I thought what might be an interesting topic tonight would be to take a look at Jesus, the man as well as God," said Donnie. "Is everyone okay with that?" The teens nodded.

"Now the reason this is so important is because of one verse in the Bible in particular. It's found in Acts 4:10-12. Who would like to read that for us? LeAnn?"

LeAnn opened her Bible and began reading: "let it be known to you all, and to all the people of Israel, that by the name of Jesus Christ of Nazareth, whom you crucified, whom God raised from the dead, by Him this man stands before you whole. This is the 'stone which was rejected by you builders, which has become the chief cornerstone.' Nor is there salvation in any other, for there is no other name under heaven given among men by which we must be saved."

"Do you see what I mean?" asked Donnie. "These verses give the answer as to why we need to know who Jesus is." Riley halfway raised his hand.

"Go, Riley. What's on your mind?"

"Well, uh, in other religions they believe that their good works can save them or if they live a good life."

"Nope, won't cut it," said Donnie. "Unless you want to throw the Bible out."

"So exactly what is it that we have to do other than to believe Jesus is Saviour?" asked Callie. "I mean I know we're to repent of our sins and accept His sacrifice and all."

"Well, Pastor Martin put it to us this way in church not too long ago. We must have faith in God and all that He says, because it's impossible to please Him if you don't. And second of all, we have to understand that power is in His blood to redeem us. Like it says in the Bible: without the shedding of blood, there is no remission of sins."

"Wow," exclaimed Riley. "Maybe you should become a minister."

"I think that's in Hebrews 9:22," added Sarah Jo. "I'll look that up." She began leafing through her Bible. "Ah, here it is: "And according to the law almost all things are purified with blood, and without shedding of blood there is no remission.""

"Thanks, Sarah Jo," acknowledged Donnie. "Back in the Old Testament they had animal sacrifice for sins, but there is no need for that any more because of Jesus Christ's sacrifice on the cross." Callie looked at Austin out of the corner of her eye and checked to see if he was still on board. Things were pretty heavy duty and she didn't want to lose him. Oddly, he sat with rapt attention as if he'd never heard these things before. Hadn't he? Then he raised his hand hesitantly.

"Austin?" said Donnie.

"Well uh, does that mean we don't take responsibility for our sins – that Christ does all that?"

"No, we have to take responsibility for having committed them which is what should bring us to Jesus to begin with. In Acts 2:38 we're told to repent and be baptized. We need to repent – to be sorry for – our sins. God will forgive us through the blood of Jesus Christ. That is essentially the gospel message. No more need for animal sacrifice, like I said. That was done away with when Jesus became our sacrifice."

Callie noted that Austin looked confused. She wondered if this discussion continued that they might lose his attention and undo all the truth that he'd learned.

"Hey," she said, "maybe we can talk about some of the things Jesus did during His ministry here on earth. I mean He set an example for all of us."

So the discussion took on a lighter note as the group contributed the noteworthy acts of Jesus. Callie knew it was no accident that they'd discussed the simple, yet awesome, truth of the mission of Jesus Christ on earth. Although she could have, she hadn't had to explain all this to Austin. It was better it came out the way it did here at the Bible study. At the end of the study they broke for refreshments and then went their separate ways. Austin asked Callie if he might walk her home, and she said yes. It was still daylight out, but she knew he wanted to walk back because he had things on his mind. They walked together in silence for a few minutes.

"So, how did you like the Bible study tonight, Austin?" she asked, hoping to draw him out.

"Truth?" he replied.

"Of course," she answered.

"I *didn't*."

"What?"

"Well, you wanted the truth," said Austin.

"What didn't you like?"

"Those verses from the Bible – about Jesus and His name."

"What was wrong with them?" asked Callie.

"They must've been taken out of context or something. I've never heard them before – or even read them myself."

"No, they were in context, and they said what they mean. Your church prob'ly doesn't read them or include them in sermons that often. Instead they prob'ly talk about Ambrose, right?"

"Hey, how did *you* know?"

"Just figured it out on my own, I guess," said Callie. They approached her house.

"Hey, you're pretty smart," said Austin.

"Thanks for walking me home."

"Not a problem. I guess I really wanted to talk to you. I'm still confused about Christ. I really don't know who He is."

"Well, you will if you keep going to the Bible studies. He's I guess what you'd call the focal point of our group – the Reason for believin'."

"We don't have anything like that in our church. I mean once a week we have a Bible study, but it's for all ages. We meet on Saturday afternoon after we eat. Our services are in the morning."

"Don't your parents wonder where you go when you come to *our* Bible studies?"

"No, cuz I kind of don't tell the truth. I tell them I need to go to the library. I guess just because I say I *need* to go there, doesn't mean I *did* go there."

"Wow! I don't like the sound of that. What if they catch you in your lie?"

"They won't. They're not suspicious. Besides this is way more important. I have to learn about Jesus Christ," declared Austin.

"Do you mind if I give you some advice – some really good advice?"

"Of course not. What is it?"

"Start reading the New Testament, beginning with the gospels. Oh, and before you do, ask God to lead and guide you into the truth," said Callie.

"That'll be a new experience for me. We mostly stay in the Old Testament and the Book of Ambrose." Callie nodded.

"Well, I'd better get in. I've got some things to do."

"Uh sure, Callie. Thanks. Bye."

"Bye, Austin."

*****

That same evening Sarah Jo called her. Callie was just about to go online to check her email.

"So, who is this Austin guy, Callie? I notice he kind of hangs with you at the Bible study." Callie wasn't quite sure how much she wanted to tell Sarah Jo about Austin, but it wouldn't be everything.

"Yeh, he's a guy I met when I was speaking to that group of young people about my experience with home school," said Callie.

"Does he go to a church around here? He kinda seems like he's out of touch," said Sarah Jo.

"Well, yes and no. I guess it's a church."

"What's the name of it?" asked Sarah Jo. Callie figured she might be telling more than she planned to but, oh well. Maybe it wouldn't hurt to have more than herself on board with this project.

"Something like Future Life Fellowship. It's not far from my place."

"I've heard of it. In fact, I've heard it's a cult," said Sarah Jo.

"Occult?" asked Callie incredulously.

"No, I said *a cult.* You know, where people believe stuff that's not Biblical." That would add up, thought Callie. The Book of Ambrose certainly couldn't be found in any Bible she'd seen – except the Alvin Barton Bible Mrs. Samuels had given her.

After that, Callie filled in the rest of the blanks about Austin, and even her encounters with Mrs. Samuels.

"I didn't want to say too much about him or Mrs. Samuels," said Callie. "Not until I knew more. I guess now I know."

"Well, you mentioned her to me, but I didn't know that much about Austin," said Sarah Jo. "I feel kinda bad for him."

"Me too. He goes to public school and he wants to play basketball, but their church won't let him."

"How come?" asked a curious Sarah Jo.

"You're not going to believe the reason." Callie explained about the uniform.

"*What?* You've got to be kidding!"

"Nope, that's what he told me," said Callie.

"Do you think maybe it's just a way that their church, uh cult, is keeping him from fitting in with the other kids?"

"I don't know," said Callie. "I just know he feels bad about it."

"Hey, can you imagine us playing, say, Hilldale and he's wearing sweats while he plays for the Pine Moor Pumas?" Callie giggled in spite of herself.

"Sarah Jo, you can't tell anyone about this," said Callie, now serious. Austin is really courageous to question his beliefs in order to learn about Jesus and the gospel."

"True, Callie. I won't say anything to anyone."

*****

A few days later Callie met up with Austin at Snackers. He said he needed to talk to her but he couldn't do it from home on the phone. After she hung up she wondered what might be on his mind. Could be anything. Did he want to tell her that he wasn't going to be able to go to Bible studies anymore?

When she entered Snackers, Austin was already seated – in a far corner. There were only a couple other people in the shop so privacy wouldn't be a problem.

"Hey Callie," said Austin as he started to get up.

"That's okay," she said. "Don't get up." One thing about Austin, he had really good manners. She sat down across from him.

"I'm glad you could come on such short notice."

"Not a problem. What's going on?" Callie noticed something different about him. There seemed to be a twinkle in his eyes where dullness had been before.

"Everything," said Austin. "I did what you said and I read the gospels – yes, right in the Alvin Barton Bible! My whole perspective has changed. I can't believe what I read."

"Really! I guess those words really spoke to your heart then," declared Callie.

"They sure did!" confirmed Austin. "Hey, can I get you a soda or something?"

"Sure, I'll have Lemon Lime Sparkle." Austin hurried back with her soda and seated himself again.

"This has been so exciting," said Austin. "But now I know I have to take the next step."

"The next step?" asked Callie as she took a sip of the clear effervescent drink.

"I figure it this way," explained Austin. "I'm going to be running into some road blocks in the not too distant future. What I mean is, I'll probably be locking horns with my parents and even the church in general. I have faith to believe that I'll get help from God if I follow what I've come to believe as being true after reading the gospels."

"And that would be...?" asked Callie.

"Well, for one thing, Jesus Christ *was* a good man, but He was so much more than that. Yes, He set certain examples for us too. I learned a lot from the parables. I'd even heard them from our church but, like I said, we mostly stayed in the Old Testament."

"So, what do you think is going to cause the most problems with your church?" Callie had decided that in addition to her own curiosity, his answers would tell her if "Project Austin" was a success. She was not disappointed.

"I learned a couple things – major things – that our church doesn't believe. First of all, Jesus is God's Son. I even learned a verse – I think. That one in John 3:16. I figured I should memorize it because that will be my proof text for what I've discovered."

"Way to go, Austin!" praised Callie. He'd gotten that part right.

"Well, that's the main thing that sticks in my mind. But the other things have to do with a backgound about Jesus as well as how He died, especially in I think it's the Book of Luke, chapter twenty-two."

"Yep, you got it," said Callie.

"I don't know how the Book of Ambrose fits into the Bible, but it's mostly vague – almost poetic – writing. It doesn't give any hard facts about who he is or was."

"Sounds to me like your spot on. That's kinda how I felt after reading the Book of Ambrose for myself," said Callie.

"So now..." said Austin as if he were choosing his words carefully, "I need to know what the next step is for me. If it has to do with Jesus Christ, I want to do it."

"I'd like to make a suggestion," said Callie. "I've been to your church already, why not come to mine? Since you have services on Saturday, it won't conflict. Could you find a reason to get out of the house?"

"Sure, I think so," replied Austin. "But they might wonder when they see me all dressed up."

"What you wear doesn't matter. God looks on the heart, not the label. Wear like what you do for teen Bible study."

"Okay, so where do I go and at what time?" Callie told him, and he wrote it down on the napkin that he'd pulled out of the chrome napkin holder on the table.

"Thanks Callie, for everything you've done," said Austin gratefully.

"Well, technically it wasn't me, but through the Holy Spirit. Let's just say that you were ready."

*****

Callie walked back home with a spring in her step. She'd never helped anyone spiritually quite like this and she had to admit, she really liked it. She planned to get to the church earlier than usual this Sunday so she could greet Austin when he arrived.

CHAPTER EIGHTEEN

Sunday finally arrived and Callie had to admit she was excited at the prospect of what the day might hold. She had told Sarah Jo that Austin would be there, but nothing beyond that. That's because there wasn't anything to tell at that point. He might come and maybe not like what he'd see and hear. Who knows if he might just get up and leave. Anything could happen.

"Hi Austin," said Callie when she saw the tall, lanky boy enter the door. His face lit up when he saw her familiar face.

"Hi Callie; finally got here." He was slightly out of breath as he confessed that he'd been running. "I didn't want to come in after church began."

"You're fine, Austin, not a problem." They only had a few minutes before the service was to begin. "Wanna sit with Sarah Jo Foster and me?"

"Sure, I mean I guess so. At our church families have to sit together. The kids can't sit with anyone else."

"Well, you'll soon find out that this isn't like your church," whispered Callie. They sat down and the service soon began. The praise and worship music was lively and inspiring.

"Wow," whispered Austin to Callie. "That gave me chills." She smiled back at him and imagined that at his church they probably played heavy, depressing music with a dirge-like quality.

The service progressed with a sermon by Pastor Martin about why we need Jesus Christ. How could he know that was just what Austin needed to hear? thought Callie. But she knew that it was God who had moved Pastor Martin to choose that subject. She became even more convinced after he'd finished and invited any and all who were convicted in their heart of their need for a Saviour, to come forward and accept Jesus Christ's sacrifice.

"All are welcome," said Pastor Martin as the music played softly in the background. "If you feel that God is knocking at the door of your heart, now is *your* time. If you are tired of your ways and are sorry for your sins come forward and invite the Lord Jesus Christ in that He may sup with you and take up residence within you. Be prepared to go with Him on the most exciting journey of your life and forever."

Callie noticed that Austin was looking around. He hesitantly got to his feet and walked down to the front. There he was greeted by several other people who began praying with him. Pastor Martin joined the small group and began to speak to Austin.

She and Sarah Jo got up and walked down to be with him and pray as well. Soon Donnie joined them. Callie could hear the low buzz of Pastor Martin's voice as the others said "amen" and "praise God". It seemed to Callie that the clock had stopped, that it was a ripple in the fabric of eternity that held Austin's salvation through the blood of Jesus Christ. As the three returned to their seats, one of the older men who'd been praying in the front told Austin that Pastor would like to see him after the service.

"You want me to hang around and wait till you're finished?" Callie whispered to Austin when they were seated.

"That's okay, I can handle it," he said with what sounded like a new found confidence. She pretty much knew what Pastor would talk to him about. It would be a welcome into the Family of God, as well as to the church. Pastor Martin finished with the benediction and people began to fellowship. Callie decided to wait for Austin and told Mom and Dad that she'd walk home. She liked being out in the fresh air especially when the day was bright and sunny as this day was.

Finally, the door to Pastor Martin's office opened and Austin appeared. He looked peaceful and confident.

"I decided to stay," said Callie. "I'm going to walk home. It's gorgeous out."

"I'll walk with you, that is, if you don't mind."

"Heck no!" exclaimed Callie. "I don't mind a bit." The two left the church, and Callie waited for Austin to speak. She didn't want to pry.

"I spose you wonder what he told me in his office," said Austin as if he could read her mind.

"Not at all," replied Callie. "Pastor usually talks to people after they've accepted Jesus as their Lord and Saviour."

"I had to tell him my circumstances, Callie. He even admitted my situation presents certain challenges, but none that God can't handle."

"That sounds like Pastor Martin. He has great faith."

"Well, I'm going to need all the faith I can get." Slowly a car pulled up beside them.

"Well, hello, Callie. Hi Austin," came a familiar voice. It was Mrs. Samuels and she had an odd look on her face. "Do you two need a ride?"

"Oh, hi Mrs. Samuels. We were just, uh, walking. It's such a beautiful day out," said Austin trying to sound casual, and before Callie could say anything. They had stopped walking so Callie knew there would be more than just a hi and good bye.

"Yes, it *is* a beautiful day," agreed Mrs. Samuels. "I just dropped Olivia off at the Swansons for a play date with their little June." Callie felt foolish just smiling pleasantly and wondering how this whole encounter would play out.

"Well, I guess we'd better be on our way," said Austin. "Thanks for stopping and asking us if we need a ride."

"Are you sure you won't take me up on that?" asked Mrs. Samuels.

"No, that's okay, but thanks," said Austin as he took a step forward. Callie followed suit.

"How about you, Callie?" persisted Mrs. Samuels.

"I'm fine with walking, thank you, Mrs. Samuels," Callie assured her.

"Well okay, if you're certain. By the way, Austin, will you let your mother know that the Women's Club will be meeting at my house next Tuesday? The date was changed because of a conflict in scheduling."

"Uh, sure, Mrs. Samuels. I will," promised Austin.

"That's a good boy," replied Mrs. Samuels condescendingly. She slowly accelerated and drove off.

"Wow!" said Callie. "Just what you needed, right?"

"Well, I think it was an opportunity to exercise my newly acquired faith and perspective."

Callie couldn't help but be concerned for Austin under the circumstances. There were bound to be fireworks over this whole matter if his parents ever found out, not to mention that church, or as Sarah Jo called it, a cult. Callie had to admit she didn't know anything about cults, nor had she ever heard her parents speak about them. She *did* know that she wouldn't have recognized one through Mrs. Samuels or, for that matter, the people who attended Future Life Fellowship. It was just that she hadn't recognized the name of that church.

After dinner Callie decided to call Sarah Jo and see what her take on the whole situation was. She explained about the walk home and that Mrs. Samuels had stopped and offered them a ride.

"Well, it's going to come out sooner or later, you know. He can't keep a secret like that indefinitely- nor should he," said Sarah Jo.

"I know, but his parents are going to ground him – for life!" exaggerated Callie.

"I don't think so. God is stronger than man," Sarah Jo reminded her.

"Well, it won't be fun for Austin under those circumstances."

"Prob'ly not but it wasn't for some of the apostles either. Some were martyred, and I don't think Austin will be facing martyrdom," said Sarah Jo.

"I hope you'll be praying for him, cuz he's gonna need it," said Callie.

"Of course I will, but this might be just what he needs to work up some spiritual muscle." Sarah Jo made a good point. She remembered how tough it was for Sarah Jo when the Fosters moved to Addison. Yes, Sarah Jo had been bullied, but she also emerged stronger for it.

The next day after her parents left for work, Callie decided to do some research on cults. She'd have to go online and simply type cults into Search and see what turned up. A knock on the front door broke her concentration. It was Mrs. Samuels and she didn't look happy. To-day she had her dull blond hair twisted in to a tight bun at the nape of her neck. Her face was tight with strain to match. Callie reluctantly opened the door.

"Callie, can we talk?" asked Mrs. Samuels curtly.

"Uh, I guess so, but we'll have to sit out on the deck. Sorry, my parents' rules. I'll meet you back there."

"Well, of all things!" muttered Mrs. Samuels as she exited the porch. Callie was on the deck as Mrs. Samuels rounded the corner of the house.

"Would you like something to drink?" asked Callie politely.

"No thanks, this isn't a social call," replied Mrs. Samuels. "The reason I'm here is because of Austin Reynolds, but you probably already know that."

"Ma'am?" asked Callie, now shifting into super-polite mode.

"Oh come now!" chided Mrs. Samuels. "Don't act like you don't know what I'm talking about."

"But I *don't*," said Callie, defending herself. It was true. She had no idea what Mrs. Samuels had heard or knew.

"Why were you and that Reynolds boy together yesterday at that time of day? I'm not ignorant. I know it's the day you go to church." Callie noticed Mrs. Samuels' face was turning an angry red.

"We were walking together. Is there anything wrong with that?"

"Walking together? *Just* walking together?" asked Mrs. Samuels. "I don't think so. I saw the two of you come out of your church."

"What? Were you *spying* on us?" asked Callie blatantly.

"And what if I was?" replied the older woman. "As a matter of fact, I was parked across the street. We look out for our own at our church."

"I've been to your church. Why is it wrong for Austin to come to mine?" asked Callie indignantly.

"You impudent little snot!" accused Mrs. Samuels. "You stay away from Austin or you'll be hearing from us." She stormed off the deck, leaving Callie in a state of shock. It sullied the whole day, but it didn't dampen her resolve to find out about cults. She knew Jesus Christ would never have acted like Mrs. Samuels had. Where was the Holy Spirit in her?

Her research on cults turned up some interesting facts, things she would never have thought of to look for. She had always thought cults were those places where people went to live in a group. She didn't know that a person's next door neighbor, who might be the nicest person in the world, could belong to a religious cult. She wondered how much Pastor Martin knew about cults and decided to ask him next Sunday. Another thing about cults that she'd read is that they're subtle. Hmmm, thought Callie, that sounded like a word that described Satan. That was kind of scary. Well, she wouldn't investigate further until she'd talked to Pastor.

Callie called Sarah Jo that night and told her about Mrs. Samuels' visit and her warning to stay away from Austin. The funny thing was, she hadn't really pursued him, any more than what Mrs. Samuels had pursued her. Besides, Austin was almost an adult. Callie figured she herself had enough on her plate without adding more.

"So, what are you going to do, Cal?" asked Sarah Jo.

"I don't know. I guess whatever God wants me to do. I'm sure not going to be afraid of Mrs. Samuels. It's like who does she think she is?"

"Well, she could make trouble for Austin, I spose," said Sarah Jo.

"Yeh, I guess, but she's not God. Actually, I just wish I'd never answered the door that day."

"Yes, but if you hadn't Austin would not have accepted Jesus Christ as his Lord and Saviour – and that is huge!"

"That's true, Sarah Jo. You got me on that one. Well, I'll have to see what Pastor Martin says."

*****

That Sunday Callie wasn't surprised to see that Austin hadn't shown up for church. It made her sad to think that he might be getting punished for having come last week. That made her all the more determined to speak to Pastor Martin. If he couldn't talk with her after church, she'd make an appointment. She told her parents that, again, she would walk home from church like last week. About a third of the way home she heard some rustling in some shrubs in a vacant lot.

"Callie!" came a hoarse voice from behind a shrub. She turned abruptly to see who it belonged to. Suddenly Austin appeared.

"Wow Austin, that didn't sound like you."

"Yeh, well, I just didn't want to scare you." He fell into stride with Callie. "Hey, can we talk?"

"Sure, I guess so. Where do you want to go?"

"Can we go to the park again? I'm not in the mood to be spied on again. I don't think Mrs. Samuels will be at the park at this time of day."

"So... what's going on?" asked Callie as they entered the park and sat on a nearby picnic table. A brook that ran through the park was babbling nearby.

"It's bad, Callie. Mrs. Samuels must've been the town crier in another lifetime. Just kidding. I don't believe in reincarnation, but if I did, that's what she'd be." Callie giggled.

"A little harsh, don't you think?"

"You don't know her like I do," said Austin. "She's one tough lady."

"Well, I don't doubt *that*," agreed Callie. "So, just what has she done?"

"She told the elders of the church and they, in turn, told my parents to rein me in."

"Were your parents angry with you?"

"Well sort of. They gave me a lecture about the evils of this world and how people who are not in our church are deceived and should be avoided when it comes to relationships – except the unavoidable ones like work or school."

"Wow," said Callie. "How do *you* feel about what they said?" Austin studied an ant that was trying to pull a miniscule crumb of food left behind on the table by picnickers. Callie just figured he needed time to answer.

"Well," he said slowly, "I know in their eyes that I've done wrong. But I don't feel that way. I think all my years in school have shown me that there are both good and bad people in this world. I'm not sure you can classify a whole group one way or the other. Individuals show their true colors sooner or later. I'd rather see them that way than throw out everyone lumped together."

"Makes sense to me." Callie also focused her attention on the ant who'd finally managed to pull the crumb to the edge of the table only to fall off with it onto the ground. "I wonder if that's how God looks at us when we try to do things ourselves."

"I don't know," said Austin. "I don't think ants have much capacity to think." They both chuckled.

"Yeh, but *we* do," said Callie. "So what are you going to do?

"I dunno. That's why I thought it might help to talk to you."

"Do you want my real feelings about this whole thing?"

"Yes, I do," said Austin emphatically. "That why I wanted to catch up to you after church."

"Well, what I think is that this problem is too big for either one of us to solve. I think we should see Pastor Martin about it. In fact, I have an appointment with him on Tuesday afternoon. Think you can make it?"

"Wait a minute, Callie," said Austin. "He's *your* pastor, not mine. How can he help *me?*"

"Let me answer your question with a question. Here goes: do you have any better suggestion as far as finding a solution?"

"Not exactly," hesitated Austin.

"I mean do you want to go to your pastor or whatever you call him?"

"Yeh sure, that's *all* I need right now," said Austin.

"Well then, come to the church on Tuesday afternoon at two o'clock," said Callie.

CHAPTER NINETEEN

Callie made sure she arrived early at the appointment with Pastor Martin. For one thing, she wanted to let Pastor know that Austin would be joining them – or at least she hoped he would.

"Do you still want me to discuss cults with you – and now Austin too?" he wondered.

"Yes. I think he can handle it especially with having the Holy Spirit. Even if he's new in the faith, God will help him understand, don't you think so?" Pastor Martin nodded in agreement.

"I most certainly do, Callie." As usual, Austin was right on time. There were greetings all around and then they sat down in Pastor Martin's office.

"I can stay for about an hour," said Austin. "Then I have to head for home."

"I'd like to begin this meeting with prayer," said Pastor Martin. When he was finished he asked Austin how things were going.

"Well, I wouldn't call them great. My parents aren't too happy with me."

"I see," said Pastor Martin. "Have they been treating you in a, well, abusive way?"

"No, nothing like that. I mean they haven't hit me or anything. They've stopped talking to me though, except only if they have to," said Austin dispiritedly.

"I see," said Pastor Martin.

"Wow Austin," whispered Callie. She couldn't imagine Mom and Dad ever doing that to her – for *any* reason.

"But, other than that you're all right?" asked the minister, his hands folded on his desk.

"Yep. I understand why they're doing it. Maybe that helps make it easier."

"Suppose you tell me what that reason is – for their not talking to you," suggested Pastor Martin

"Well, in their eyes," Austin started out slowly, "they see me as having broken the rules."

"In what way?" asked Pastor Martin.

"Well, we've been taught to be separate from the world – to not mix in with them."

"And how do they define that word 'world'?"

"I guess you could say the world is anyone outside of the church," answered Austin.

"What church specifically?"

"Well, I guess our church, at least that's how I always took it," said Austin.

"Just by that statement alone you've just provided one of the identifiers of what a cult is," explained Pastor Martin. "It's referred to as elitism, or the notion of superiority. How much do you know about cults, son?"

"Uh... what's a cult?" asked Austin sheepishly.

"Well, the definition I'm going to use is that of a religious system with unorthodox or extremist views, beliefs or practices. It is often accompanied by a charismatic religious leader."

"You think that's what Future Life Fellowship is?" asked a horrified Austin.

"I'll tell you what, Austin," said Pastor Martin. "I'm going to let you make that determination for yourself. Then when you've studied things out, I'd like you to contact me and we can resume this discussion. Same for you, Callie. Now I'd like to give you your assignment. I took the liberty of printing out a set of eight criteria for what defines a cult. You could have found it yourself by typing 'cult; definition of' in Search on your computer, but I've saved you the time." Pastor Martin handed each of them some printed sheets of paper. "Now, go do your assignment and we will talk soon. Austin, in your case, I suggest you keep this paper to yourself, for the time being anyway. If you have any questions along the way, just give me a call here." Callie and Austin thanked Pastor Martin and walked out.

"Wow," said Austin. "I'm trying to wrap my head around this. I have a feeling this is really going to be an eye opener."

"I know," said Callie. "Pastor Martin gets to the bottom of things." They reached the park.

"Here's where we part ways, Callie. I have to get home as soon as possible so as not to raise any suspicions as to where I've been. I'll try and call later."

"Okay. I'll pray that it all goes well for you at home."

When Callie got home she decided to give Sarah Jo a call. This was just too big of a thing to keep to herself.

*****

"Hi, Sarah Jo. It's me. I just got back from seeing Pastor Martin. Austin was there too."

"So, how did it go?"

"Well, okay for me," answered Callie. "Maybe for Austin not so much."

"How do you figure?"

"Well, for one thing, I think he's going to get a crash course in Cults 101."

"What do you mean?"

"Pastor Martin gave us both sheets listing identifiers for a cult."

"Hmmm... interesting," said Sarah Jo. "Well, at least Austin will have it in black and white."

"Yep. This may be where the rubber meets the road."

Callie decided to give Mom a head start on dinner. Fried chicken sounded good and the cut up fresh chicken was already in the refrigerator. She liked to experiment with recipes but she decided she'd just dip the pieces in flour seasoned with salt and pepper and fry them till brown, then bake them the rest of the way until they were done. All the while her mind was on Austin and what he was discovering with the information Pastor Martin had given him. She had yet to look at hers. She'd save it for after dinner.

Dinner time was always a chance to catch up in the Morris household, but tonight Callie was keeping her day to herself – at least the part about Austin. She wanted to make sure that what she said was accurate and that would require looking over the information Pastor Martin had given her on the subject of cults.

"So, how was *your* day, Callie?" asked Dad after telling her and Mom what he'd accomplished at work.

"Well, I've been doing some research but I'd rather not say too much until it's complete. Then I'll let you and Mom know about it."

"Ah, being mysterious, are we?" asked Dad with a twinkle in his eye.

"Can you give us a hint, Callie?" asked Mom playfully.

"Not just yet. I'll be done soon. Then I'll share."

"That works for me," said Dad.

"Me too," added Mom. Callie was glad her parents didn't push for information. They didn't pry like some parents. They trusted her and that brought out the best in her. She wouldn't let them down. That night, after she helped Mom with the dishes, she went to her room to delve into the information on cults that Pastor Martin had given her. Callie found that it wasn't easy reading but, then, she really hadn't expected it to be. It was written by a doctor so that may have explained the technical jargon. By the time she'd finished, she was convinced that Austin was in for a shock, that is, if he was honest.

Future Life Fellowship, at least from what she could tell, had at least four characteristics of a cult, maybe more. As if on cue, the phone rang. It was Austin.

"Callie, I had to call you," announced the agitated voice at the other end.

"You read those info sheets from Pastor Martin," stated Callie matter-of-factly.

"*Wow... did I!*"

"You okay?"

"I am now. At least someone's telling me the truth," said Austin.

"Well, God always has been, but we often just believe what we're told by people around us. You get the straight stuff from His Word."

"No kidding!" declared Austin. "I guess I was reading the wrong version of it. I definitely was listening to the wrong people."

"Where are you calling from?" asked Callie.

"From home. My parents are at the neighbors. My father is helping with a repair on their pickup truck and my mother went along to visit the man's wife."

"Did they just leave?"

"No, a while ago, so I'd better hang up soon. Then I have to dial in a wrong number – I'll make one up – so that when my father comes back and redials the number it won't be yours."

"Wow, they really *don't* trust you, do they?" asked Callie incredulously.

"Nope, no one trusts anyone in this cult I'm part of – not even family."

*****

It was discouraging for Callie to learn that cults exist in order to deceive trusting people who might otherwise have become true believing Christians. Not that it was ever too late if they were still drawing breath, but just that these vulnerable people let others program their minds with their false beliefs. According to what she'd read, there was usually some truth mixed in – just enough to make their systems seem believable. Of course, in the case of children born into a cult this was all they ever knew. She noticed there was a bibliography with a book titled *Programmed From Birth* that she just might want to check out from the library. Austin would fit into that category. What he'd been taught about God – and Ambrose for that matter – was the only truth he'd known about God's identity.

Austin had told her that he needed to talk to Pastor Martin as soon as possible now that he was convinced he was in a religious cult. He needed advice from someone more experienced than himself, he told Callie. She said she would meet him at Pastor's office, if he didn't mind. No, he didn't mind; in fact he welcomed her support. So, that next day the two found themselves once again sitting on the other side of the desk from Pastor Martin.

"So Austin, now that you're convinced that Future Life Fellowship is a cult, do you have any ideas as to what you're going to do next?" Pastor Martin's forehead was furrowed with lines of concern.

"Not really. That's why I came to you." Callie wondered what her minister might say next.

"Well, I think we should start by thinking this through, which I'm pretty sure you have a number of times already. Since you called me, I've been mulling this over as well. I've come up with only a couple of ways to handle this situation," said Pastor Martin. Austin looked up.

"You mean there's actually a way for me to deal with this?"

"Son, there's always a way to deal with things. Even doing nothing at all is a way people deal with things – not a very good way, but a way."

"Here's the first way and perhaps the most obvious solution," explained Pastor Martin. "Simply tell the truth." Austin looked visibly shaken.

"Uh, that's not an option, sir," stammered Austin. "I mean that would be like starting World War III."

"Well, the other thing you can do – and *should* do in any event- is to keep praying and let God guide you. Now, I personally don't know how I would remain in the cult and sit through their teachings knowing what I'd learned in terms of the truth."

"Me either," said Callie barely audibly.

"I *did* find one thing in particular very helpful in terms of my searching out truth on this subject. More than one source said the one major thing lacking in a cult is love. Therefore we need to be willing to show love to those who are in a cult." Austin nodded.

"How you deal with this," continued Pastor Martin, "is largely up to you. I'm at a disadvantage in that I don't know these people like you do. That's *your* advantage."

"Or *dis*advantage," said Austin, his voice sinking.

"Austin, you can never forget that you have the truth on your side, and more importantly, God," reminded Pastor Martin.

"True," agreed Callie. It appeared to her that Austin looked more confused than ever. She knew he was at a crossroads that he didn't want to enter.

"May we pray?" suggested Pastor Martin. His prayer was direct and to the point in terms of urgency. When he was finished, both Callie and Austin thanked him.

Once outside and on their way home, the serious discussion began. Austin voiced his concerns.

"I just don't know what to do, Callie. I mean this is life-changing stuff here."

"I know," replied Callie. "Pretty heavy duty."

"My parents could make life really miserable for me if I tell them any of this."

"Yes, but don't forget the power of God factor. It could make all the difference. Remember David and Goliath. I presume you've read about them."

"Of course – hasn't *everyone?*

"I don't know. Maybe some cults skip over it," said Callie.

"I need to formulate a plan, something workable," declared Austin somberly. He walked in silence for a few minutes. "Have you got time to go to the park?" asked Austin.

"I have a little extra time," said Callie. "Why?"

"Because I need your help," said Austin all too quickly.

"Not really. You need God's help more. I might steer you wrong."

"Well, you can just listen then, because I can't just keep going on as I have been." They reached the park and sat down on a bench that was shaded from the sun.

"You know, I *can* give you one bit of advice – good advice," said Callie.

"What's that?" asked Austin.

"Well, you sought wise counsel and got it from Pastor Martin. So

I'd choose what he offered in terms of advice. I think God will honor that more readily than ignoring it and coming up with something on your own."

"You make a good point, Callie. Okay, so I either tell who – my parents, Bishop Jude Bartholomew? Who?"

"Well, I would think your parents. They'd want to know and they are your flesh and blood, after all. I know I can tell my parents anything."

"Yes – *your* parents, not mine. I can't tell them just anything. Hey, I've got an idea. It certainly couldn't hurt."

"What's that?" asked Callie.

"What if we ran this by your folks. They're believers, right?"

"Of course! Well, I guess it couldn't hurt anything."

"Great!" said Austin. "Will you ask them about it – sooner rather than later?"

"Sure. When I get home. And don't worry, I won't tell them about your situation. I'll leave that to you."

"Thanks, Callie! You're a real friend," declared Austin.

*****

Callie approached Mom and Dad during dinner. They were usually relaxed by then and able to take on new information.

"So you want us to hear something Austin has on his mind?" confirmed Dad.

"Yes, and maybe give any advice you might have."

"I don't know, Callie," said Dad dubiously. "He's not my son. I wouldn't want to go over his parents' heads if my advice would be different from theirs."

"Well, even if you would just hear him out. Then tell him if you can say anything or not," said Callie.

"You father *does* make a good point, Callie. After all, Austin has his own parents to discuss things with."

"It's not like that though," protested Callie. "Not all parents are like you and Dad."

"I'll tell you what, Callie," said Dad reaching for another ear of corn. "I'll hear what he has to say, but I won't promise to advise him. If it's something his parents need to know, he'll have to go to them for advice. Fair enough?"

"Yes sir," said Callie. She knew Dad meant business.

It was decided that Austin would come over the next night. He'd been so anxious for Callie's answer that he called soon after her and her parents' discussion. Callie heard the relief in his voice when the call was drawing to a close.

"See you tomorrow night, Callie, and thanks again. I'm really anxious to see if your parents have anything to say."

*****

The following night, as could be expected, Austin was right on time. Mom and Dad were in good spirits in spite of the gravity of what the situation might yield.

"Come on in, young man," invited Dad. "Have a seat." Austin thanked him and sat down. Mom sat on the periphery of the living room as did Callie. They didn't want to distract Austin as he explained his dilemma. When he finished, Callie noticed the look on Dad's face. It was one she didn't recognize.

"Well son," said Dad finally, "that's quite a predicament. I have to say I've never heard of anything quite like it." Austin looked down as if ashamed.

"I just don't know what to do, Mr. Morris."

"What do you think about all this, Amanda?" She just shook her head.

"Well, you said you talked to Pastor Martin about it and he gave you some advice, as you mentioned. I'd say work from that and put it in God's hands," said Callie's father.

"One thing I know," said Austin. "I can't go on pretending that Future Life Fellowship is the place for me. They don't preach Jesus Christ there. It's all about Ambrose."

"I don't know who Ambrose is, son, but there is only one Saviour and we need Him. His name is Jesus Christ," said Dad. "You realize that now which is why Ambrose is irrelevant to you, right?"

"Yes sir, I do. Maybe that's why I have to just be up front about this with them and take whatever consequences come my way. I can't go on pretending to believe a lie," said Austin.

"Well then, I think you have your answer," said Dad.

"Callie, if you don't hear from me for a while, just figure I'm grounded for months with no access to a phone," said Austin as he looked in her direction. Callie didn't know what to say.

"Let me tell you this one thing, Austin," said Dad in a somber tone of voice.

"Parents or not, if they lay a hand on you or something like that, you have the right to protect yourself in which case I would say flee from the premises. I have a feeling that won't happen, but I've heard about cults in which it's all too common."

"I don't think that would happen," said Austin. "Of course I've never questioned the beliefs of Future Life Fellowship before either." Austin got up from where he was sitting and Callie followed suit from her chair and walked with him to the door.

"I'll be praying for you, Austin," said Callie.

"We *all* will," added Dad. "Good night, Austin."

"Good night, sir and thank you. 'Night Mrs. Morris. Bye Callie. I'll try to call when I can."

CHAPTER TWENTY

Two weeks had gone by since Austin had been over to see the Morrises and Callie was worried. She figured she'd have at least gotten even a brief phone call. When two weeks became a month, she knew something was very wrong. Austin had been staying in touch regularly and now she heard nothing from him. She told Sarah Jo about it and her friend agreed that it was certainly something to pray about, and enlisted Wendy and Laura in Addison for that also. After church on Sunday, Pastor Martin took Callie aside and asked how Austin was doing. Callie told him she didn't know since she hadn't heard from him. Pastor Martin's face registered concern.

"I thought this might happen," he mumbled to himself. Callie didn't know what he meant but she felt it was not the right time to question her pastor about it. Austin's noticeable lack of communication was the topic of discussion at lunch when she and her family got home.

"Don't worry about it, dear," said Mom who could be counted on to always be sensible. "It's in God's hands."

"I'll tell you what," said Dad. "If you don't hear from him by the end of the week, we'll try and find out what's going on."

"Okay Dad," said Callie, relieved.

They didn't have to wait until the end of the week for that. It came as soon as Monday morning. Mom and Dad were at work. Callie went out to get the mail. There it was – an envelope with a hastily scrawled name, *her* name, and address. No return address. The stamp in the corner looked as though it had been pried off another envelope and pasted on this one. In spite of its shabby condition, it had reached its destination. Callie hastily opened the envelope. Inside there was but one word scribbled in block letters: Help!

Callie panicked and phoned Mom. When she explained what had happened, Mom seemed puzzled.

"Are you sure this is from Austin?"

"Yes Mom. I *know* it is!"

"Calm down, Callie. I'm going to call your father and see what he thinks. I'll call you right back." The minutes seemed to drag into hours when the phone rang.

"Hello," said Callie in a quivering voice.

"Callie," said Mom. "I told your father and he said he'd be right home. He said it sounded like something serious."

"Okay Mom; thanks." She held the piece of paper in her hand, not knowing what to think. What had happened? Was Austin okay? Her imagination ran wild but she felt that she had run through all possible scenarios except the one that really happened.

Callie heard Dad drive up and she went out to meet him. She handed the scrap of paper to him.

"Get in the car, Callie. We're going to get to the bottom of this."

"Are you going to Austin's? Cuz if you are, I don't know where he lives."

"No, we're going to the authorities. They'll know what to do." It didn't take long to get to the police station. Callie and her father found themselves in an office sitting across from Sergeant Pete Sloan.

"Now, suppose you tell me all that you know," Sergeant Sloan addressed Callie after her father gave the officer the backstory. Callie hated to do it, but she knew she must, cult information and all.

"How do you know it's a cult?" asked Sergeant Sloan. Callie went on to explain the various characteristics of a cult, basically the information Pastor Martin had given her.

"Well, I'll tell you something, young lady. I don't think I'm in a position to judge what's a cult or not, but I *do* respond to a call for help such as what you've provided here. We'll have someone look into it. In the meantime, I suggest you go out and try and enjoy this beautiful summer day." With that, the officer rose signaling that their meeting had come to an end. Callie wanted to ask him questions, but she knew better than to do so.

"Will you keep us informed?" asked Dad. "This young man is a friend of the family."

"I can't promise that. If the boy's a minor, we try to keep that information confidential," said Sergeant Sloan.

Callie and her father discussed Austin's "disappearance" at length. She fixed a sandwich for her father, but she herself wasn't hungry.

"Here Dad," she said as she placed the plate in front of him.

"Thanks honey. I don't have time to eat it now, but I'll take it with me. I've got a project going on at work that I've got to get back to. A personal emergency request will only get you so far."

"Sure Dad. Thanks for knowing what to do – and doing it." She walked to the front door with him.

"Pray for Austin, Cal. I have a feeling he's going to need it. Oh, and you might want to call Pastor Martin and catch him up to date. I'm sure he'd appreciate that and will want to be praying for him also. See you later." He got into the car and sped off into the direction of work.

Wow, thought Callie. Just wow! Who would've guessed all of this would end up being a police matter? She decided she'd go online just to get her mind off of things. After that she'd call Pastor Martin. As she sat down to the computer she heard a frenzied knocking on the door. The loud, insistent knocking jarred her, and Callie decided to see who it was. It could be an emergency – it could be Austin!

Her hopes were soon dashed.

"Answer the door! I know you're in there," came the all-too-familiar voice of Fern Samuels. "Open up this minute!" It was a temptation to just yell back "Go away!" but wisdom got the better of her and she kept quiet. The knocking continued.

"Listen *you*! You got Austin and the Reynolds family into a whole lot of trouble and you're going to answer for it. The police were over there and now Family Services is involved. Mrs. Reynolds told me herself when she called for prayer. And you're responsible for it, you teenage troublemaker! You'd better be praying to your God about this because you're going to need all the help you can get."

Callie noticed that this woman - "supposedly" a good Christian woman – shook her fist at the door and turned on her heel and left. Callie was shaking. She'd never seen a look like that on the face of any-one. She didn't know if she should call Mom or just keep it to herself. One call in a day to Mom at her job was enough. She'd just wait until Mom got home from work. One thing she could do, though, was to call Pastor Martin. She would *definitely* do that.

Pastor Martin didn't seem surprised by what Callie had told him. In fact, he acted like he was expecting her call.

"It's okay, Callie. People get ugly – literally and figuratively – when they get angry. I guess that's why they say the devil is so ugly."

"Pastor Martin, what do you think happened to Austin?" asked Callie. There was a moment's silence, then she heard a sigh through the phone.

"Well Callie," said Pastor Martin as he chose his words carefully. "You're old enough to know how the world works. I was rather afraid this would happen, but I couldn't stop it from happening either. It had to be Austin's choice."

"What do you mean? I don't understand."

"Well, from everything you told me about, including the note, Austin apparently chose to tell his parents the truth and the fact that he had asked Jesus into his life and became a believer. What came after, I fear, is what resulted in that note. His parents must have punished him in such a way that he needed to reach out for help. If he'd had a way to contact you other than the way he did, he no doubt would have."

"I can't believe his parents would do something to hurt him," said Callie incredulously.

"Well, unfortunately, in his parents' skewed view of things they probably figured they were protecting him. We don't know the details so it's just speculation."

"What do *you* think happened to him, Pastor Martin?"

"I hesitate to say because I have no way of knowing. However, I will say this – and please don't quote me on this – it sounds like maybe Austin was locked in his room or some other room. Some way he was able to make it to the mail box with that letter to you, maybe at night or something."

"Yes, he lives out on the edge of town so the mailbox is probably at the end of his driveway," added Callie.

"When the authorities saw that note you and your father brought to them, they were obliged to check things out to make sure the law wasn't being broken. They must've seen some wrong had been committed against Austin and, since he's still a minor, had him taken into protective custody by Family Services."

"Yikes! No wonder Mrs. Samuels was so mad at me."

"You did nothing wrong," assured Pastor Martin. "In fact, you did everything right. Who knows, you may have saved Austin's life."

During dinner Callie told her parents everything that had happened, including Mrs. Samuels' tirade outside the front door. As she explained the incident to her parents, Dad's face became noticeably troubled.

"I don't like this, Amanda. I don't like this at all. Callie, you did right by not answering the door. Who knows what she would've done had you opened it." Callie looked to see what Mom's reaction was; it wasn't good.

"Well, all I can say is that she'd best not come knocking on our door again. She's not welcome here."

"I agree," said Dad. "If there's any more of that, I'll get legal advice. It may be necessary to get a restraining order."

After dinner, and when the dishes were loaded into the dishwasher, Callie called Sarah Jo. She told her friend everything that had happened so far.

"Oh my gosh!" exclaimed Sarah Jo. "What do you think has happened to Austin?"

"I don't know, but if he's away from that group of people he's much better off."

"Maybe so, but that's his family we're talking about here. He might not miss the group, but his parents are flesh and blood."

"I know," said Callie. "I can't even imagine being away from my parents like that."

"Well, if they mistreated you, you would. And that's no doubt what happened to Austin."

*****

The very next day, about mid-morning the phone rang. She half expected it would be Mom checking up on her to make sure she was okay, but it wasn't. It was Austin.

"Hi Austin," said Callie. "Are you okay? Where are you?"

"Chill, Callie," said Austin. "I'm fine."

"What happened? I mean since we last talked," asked Callie.

"Well, I'm not at home anymore."

"Where are you then?" she asked.

"I'm with a foster family. They're real nice."

"Wow! What happened that you ended up in foster care?" asked Callie.

"Well, I decided to tell my parents the truth. I figured that was the place to start.

I wasn't ready to face Bishop Jude Bartholomew," admitted Austin. "I prayed about my situation all the way from your house back home."

"Then what happened?" asked Callie.

"Well, the folks were suspicious about me being gone and asked where I'd been."

"And...?"

"So I told them I had gone to get advice on a personal matter. They said, 'A personal matter, and you couldn't come to us?' I told them, not *this* time."

"Then what happened?" asked Callie with baited breath.

"They got angry – I mean real angry," said Austin. So I figured I might as well start at the beginning and tell them everything – and I did."

"Oh wow!" said Callie.

"Yep! They really went ballistic. I thought my dad was gonna give me a taste of his belt like he did when I was a kid."

"You're kidding!" said Callie incredulously.

"Nope. So he said, 'Follow me.' And I did. He took me downstairs to the basement."

"I don't know if I want to hear any more of this," said Callie.

"I'll stop if you want me to," said Austin.

"No," said Callie. "I'd rather hear it from you than someone else later." So Austin continued, revealing that he'd been banished to the basement until he got some 'sense in his head' as his father had put it. The door was locked at the top of the stairs. And that was that.

"So, how did you get that letter to me?" asked Callie.

"Well, after praying – being locked up can cause you to become very good at fervent prayer – I checked the wood chute that had been nailed shut. You know, where they put the logs through when they used wood heat years ago?"

"Yes, go on," answered Callie.

"Well I found an old hammer in the basement. My dad had a few tools down there for repairs and stuff. So I took that wood cover off and snuck out to the mailbox with my letter to you. I just had to hope they didn't notice the flag was up, but that was the chance I had to take."

"Apparently, they didn't see it," concluded Callie.

"Right."

"So, how long will you be with your new family?" asked Callie.

"Well, technically, I guess just until I graduate. Then I'm pretty much on my own."

"What about your parents? What happens with them?"

"That's the hard part," confessed Austin. They have a court appearance coming up so now they have a lawyer. No one tells me much about this, but I *am* worried about them. I know that they were just following their consciences about this. It's what they've been taught by Future Life Fellowship. If there's a guilty party here it should be the Fellowship."

"Will they stand by your parents on this?"

"No way!" replied Austin emphatically. "They don't like to get involved with what they call the goings-on of the world."

"Wow! So in a way, it's 'the world' that's standing by you and watching out for you," said Callie.

"Yep, pretty much."

"Do you get to come and go as you want at your new place?" asked Callie.

"Well, I just got here, so I don't know. But I imagine I'll have to have accountability."

"Meaning...?"

"Well, just meaning that I'll need to let them know where I'm going. It's not like getting permission but I can't just pretend that I'm free to do what I want and go where I want."

"I guess that makes sense," said Callie.

"Well, I'd better go now. I'll talk to you soon," said Austin.

"Okay, bye."

Callie was glad that Austin had called, but disheartened that his family had turned against him, not to mention his church. And now it appeared his family would be in trouble too. Still, the way they handled things was all wrong, to her way of thinking. Austin just wanted to do what was right. He didn't deserve to be treated like a prisoner. How could his own father lock him up in the basement? That seemed rather uncivilized to her.

Callie's parents wanted to know if she'd heard from Austin, so she told them what she knew. They were taken aback by what they heard, if being speechless was any indication.

"Well, I'm just telling you what Austin told me," said Callie apologetically that evening after supper. She almost hated to mention it since her parents were relaxing out on the deck with iced tea.

"Dear," said Mom, "you have nothing to do with it. You were just being a friend. It's unfortunate what happened but it has nothing to do with you."

"I can't believe there are people like this in our small town," grumbled Dad.

"I think you'd better give this whole thing a break for awhile, Callie," said Mom. "It's really negative to think about – and discuss – for any period of time."

"Okay," replied Callie who was more than willing to put it out of her mind for awhile. I think I'll call Sarah Jo and see what she's up to."

"Good idea, and try to keep off the subject of Austin," said Mom.

*****

The phone call resulted in making plans for the following day. She and Sarah Jo decided to meet at the park and have a picnic lunch. Each would bring their own and save money at the same time. The weather looked to be fine according to the local report on television. It sounded like fun, thought Callie. The next day Callie made a lunch for herself and a little extra in case Sarah Jo wanted to sample some of what she would be eating. Once at the park, she saw her friend approaching in the distance and waved to her. She got a wave in return.

"Hey Cal. Wow, our timing is right on!"

"Yep. It sure is. How about that table under the tree there?"

"Looks okay to me," said Sarah Jo. "I brought a couple big cloth napkins we use at picnics that we can put under each of our lunches. You never know who might have sat on the table." She fished them out of her backpack along with her lunch.

"Good thinking." Callie recalled that it might have been her and Austin who'd been sitting there while at the park.

"So, what's new?" asked Sarah Jo, as she opened up the waxed paper wrapping on her sandwich. "Oh wait! You wanna say the blessing?"

"Sure," said Callie and she launched into words of thanksgiving over their lunches. "In His name we ask this... amen."

"Amen."

"Well, there's stuff that's been going on, but I'm sposed to talk about fun stuff," giggled Callie. She took a bite of her cheese sandwich. She noticed Sarah Jo had peanut butter and jelly on whole wheat. Her mom no doubt had been baking. Before she could say anything more she saw a familiar lanky frame headed their way.

"Hey, is three a crowd?" called out none other than Austin who was carrying a basketball in one hand.

"Hi Austin," said Sarah Jo.

"Hey Austin," Callie greeted him.

"Just came down to get some practice in. I'm going to be on the team this year," said Austin jubilantly.

"Wow! That's great," exclaimed Callie.

"Hey, do you want to sit down with us and have something to eat? I sure don't need all that I brought," confessed Sarah Jo.

"Me neither," added Callie. "In fact, I packed a little extra, just in case."

"Are you sure?" asked Austin who gratefully accepted.

"Sure, we're sure," said Callie in no uncertain terms. "Do you like cheese sandwiches?

"I like anything but pickle and marmalade sandwiches," joked Austin. That brought laughs all around. As they ate lunch, Austin described his new temporary family. He confessed that he missed his parents and that he missed some of the people from Future Life Fellowship, but he didn't miss going to their services one bit. Nor did he miss their rules. Sure, there were times when guilt plagued him a little, but he didn't dwell on it.

"So, what's going to happen to your folks?" asked Sarah Jo.

"I don't know too much at this point," said Austin, "but I don't think they're in too much trouble. I heard that their lawyer will be making a case for them being first time offenders and just an error in judgment on their part."

"So, will you have to go back and live with them?" asked Callie.

"I'm not sure. I guess time will tell. They're doing an investigation of Future Life Fellowship to see if anything like this has happened before."

"So, how does all of this make *you* feel?" asked Sarah Jo. Austin was not quick to answer. Finally he spoke.

"Well, I can't say that I'm happy about it. It's unfortunate it had to come to this. But I also know my dad and how stubborn he is. He would've left me in the basement till I cracked and gave in. - which I couldn't do because of what I now believe."

"What about your mother?" asked Callie.

"Oh, she stands right behind my dad on stuff. That's what the women are taught in the Fellowship. If she went against my father, she'd probably have ended up in the basement with me." Both girls giggled until they realized that Austin was serious.

"Oh my gosh!" exclaimed Sarah Jo. "You're serious!" Austin looked back at her, puzzled.

"Of course I am. You think I'd joke about something like that?"

"Wow," said Callie softly. She couldn't believe it. It would be wrong to keep an animal in a damp old basement, let alone people, and certainly not loved ones. Callie wondered if there was even any love within Austin's family – or for that matter, Future Life Fellowship.

"Hey, let's not talk about this any more. I kinda crashed your picnic so I think I'm going to go shoot some hoops which is why I came here in the first place. Thanks for sharing lunch, Callie and Sarah Jo." He loped off in the direction of the basketball court.

"Hey Austin," called out Sarah Jo. Austin turned around. "We'll be praying for you and your situation." Austin raised his hand in acknowledgment and continued on his way.

CHAPTER TWENTY ONE

Austin's family had made the news in the little town of Pine Moor. It wasn't that news was so hard to come by but the fact that the offense was so great. You didn't just lock up your child in some area of your home – for *any* reason. There would have been no reason that would have been acceptable – and yet Austin's father had elected to do that. But beyond that was the fact that other similar instances were turning up within Future Life Fellowship within the state. This type of behavior was unacceptable if it happened between two adults, let alone a minor child, according to Mom.

"Did they say anything about Austin, Dad?" asked Callie.

"No, there's no mention of him by name since he's a minor," said Dad as he loosely folded the paper and put it next to his breakfast plate that had held pancakes earlier.

"What do you think will happen?" asked Callie.

"I think this is very serious business," said Mom as she poured another cup of coffee into Dad's cup and then her own.

"See, here's the thing, Cal," said Dad. "In God's economy, children are on loan to us to raise on His behalf. Someday you'll understand that when you have children of your own. When anger or an inflated sense of authority take over, someone's likely to get hurt and it's usually the children. God doesn't take kindly to that."

"Yes, but what if children really disobey?" asked Callie.

"Well, the situation with Austin was not really disobedience," said Mom. "It has to do with that cult they're in. Unfortunately, their god *is* the cult and it's distorted their view of the true God."

"That's true," agreed Dad. "And you can't just say anyone who believes differently than you is a cult. But I can tell you, anywhere there's abuse, it is not God.

*****

Callie was amazed at how much she'd learned about cults without really having known they even existed before she met Mrs. Samuels and especially Austin. Oh, she'd heard the word before like once when there were problems that involved the authorities on a large scale. It was on the national news, so it was big news. But in a little town such as theirs? Unheard of.

That Sunday at church Pastor Martin spoke on the subject of cults. Austin, who had begun attending church there, bravely spoke about his personal experience. Callie noted that he didn't go into great detail which probably had to do in part with time constraints. He also seemed to want to make the point that his parents were not "bad" people, but only doing what the cult had taught them to do.

Pastor Martin spoke after Austin was finished.

"So you see, brothers and sisters, Satan will use any means at his disposal to break up families and try and damage the fabric of our society. He doesn't care one whit what is happening to Austin's family right now. So, I'm going to ask you to include Austin and his family in your prayers. Let's see what kind of miracle will result." After church was dismissed, a considerable group of people gathered around Austin with their questions. Watching from her vantage point near the door, it was right then and there that Callie decided that she wanted to major in college courses that would teach her to help other people, especially those caught up in false religious cults. She'd have to have specialized training for that, but her college major would be social work.

At dinner she told her parents of her plan. They both seemed surprised but not resistant to the idea.

"It's just that the enemy tries to take on a religious appearance as just one more way to hurt people. It's like people want to be able to trust what they believe spiritually, then he wrecks it all."

"That is true, Callie," said Dad. "Nothing is sacred – *literally* – to him. It's always open season on Christians."

"I think you've made a wise choice, dear," said Mom.

*****

Callie and her three good friends – Sarah Jo, Wendy and Laura – decided to have one last get-together before summer was over and it was time to go back to school. She could hardly wait to tell them of her decision in terms of a career choice. Mom and Dad approved the sleepover and soon she was planning it, along with some help from Sarah Jo.

"What kind of food should we have?" asked Callie after church the next Sunday.

"Hey, how about tacos? Who doesn't like them?" replied Sarah Jo as they stood near the back of the church.

"Sarah Jo, can I ask you something kinda stupid?"

"Sure, as long as you don't *call* me stupid." They both laughed.

"Well, I think this problem with cults is bigger than the church community realizes. In other words, we Christians are all pretty trusting, don't you think?"

"And your point is?" asked Sarah Jo.

"Well, the more we can spread the word, the better. I was thinking it would be kinda cool if we could ask Austin here for tacos and let him tell his story to Wendy and Laura."

"Hmmm... and he leaves right after dinner, right? Cuz I want to catch up with Wendy and Laura, and have some fun."

"Of course! What did you think?" asked Callie incredulously.

"Then let's do it," said Sarah Jo. "I think it would be good for Wendy and Laura to hear about it."

The girls planned their sleepover for Friday night, but Wendy and Laura would be leaving on Monday afternoon when the bus would take them back to Addison. Callie's mother drove to the bus depot to pick the girls up, with an anxious Callie searching to see if her friends were waiting outside. There they were! They must have just gotten there. The car came to a stop and Callie jumped out of the car and ran to greet Wendy and Laura.

"Hi guys!" she called out.

"Hey," answered Wendy. Laura waved feebly under the weight of her back pack

"How was the bus trip?" asked Callie.

"Kinda boring," confessed Wendy. "Or it would've been if Laura hadn't been along." Laura flashed her winning smile. They got into the car and began chattering.

"Welcome, Wendy and Laura," said Mrs. Morris. "Glad you could come visit us."

"Hi!" said the girls in unison and then resumed their animated conversation with Callie. After they had set up their sleeping bags in Callie's room, Wendy and Laura followed Callie downstairs. Callie's mother had announced the arrival of Sarah Jo who was waiting at the bottom of the stairs. Wendy and Laura hugged their friend and were hugged in return.

"It's so good to see you guys," said Sarah Jo.

"Yeh, same here," said Laura.

"No kidding," Wendy chimed in.

"Hey, wanna help put the taco fixings together?" asked Callie. "Then we can eat. Oh, by the way, we're going to have our own guest for dinner." The conversation stopped. "Austin is coming by. I think I told you about him."

"Yeh, isn't he a little weird?" asked Laura.

"Maybe," answered Sarah Jo, "but when you hear what he's been through, then you'll know why."

"Right, we'll let him tell his story in his own words," said Callie as she put the bowl of shredded cheese on the table. Mom and Dad were having their own dinner later, since it would allow privacy for the girls and Austin who had just arrived. "Wendy and Laura, this is Austin Reynolds."

"Hi," said Austin to the group.

"Callie told us you have a story to tell," said Wendy. Austin nodded.

"It must be *some* story that she'd invite you over when *we're* here," said Laura. "Oops, sorry. Didn't mean it to sound that way."

"That's okay," replied Austin as he balanced his tacos on a paper plate. "It was a learning experience for sure."

"Let's go out to the deck to eat," suggested Callie. "We can always come back in if we want more." She set her food down on the table and went back in the house to get a pitcher of lemonade with ice cubes floating and clinking on top. "Sarah Jo, can you bring out the glasses?"

"That's okay," said Austin. "I'm closer. I'll get 'em." Once the group was situated and a blessing was said, Callie asked Austin if he'd like to tell the Addison girls about himself.

"Sure," he said affably. "After I finish these tacos."

"Oh, sorry," apologized Callie. "I'm just so anxious for Wendy and Laura to hear your story."

"Not a problem," answered Austin as he bit into his last taco. "In the meantime why don't you two tell me about your experience of finding Jesus."

"That might take a while," said Wendy, "but I'll try and give you the condensed version." She proceeded to tell the group about the tornado and her father and the beginning of the Heaven Club. When she finished, Austin sat there wide-eyed.

"Wow!"

"Yep," said Wendy. "It's amazing what God can do through anyone who has given their life to Him and believed in Jesus as His Son and what He has done by saving them. Tell him *your* story, Laura." Laura did. Austin was equally impressed. By then he had finished his tacos and was ready to talk about his experience. Both Wendy and Laura couldn't believe what they were hearing. Laura's jaw dropped open.

"You're kidding!" she said when Austin told about not being able to play basketball because of the cult's dress code.

"I wish I was cuz if I *was* kidding I might be a star player on the team at high school by now." Both Wendy and Laura stared at Austin in disbelief.

"Why would anyone get themselves into that kind of outfit?" asked Wendy.

"I mean it's sure not a church."

"No, it isn't," replied Austin, "but it may seem like one at first. And, by the way, it's not something people get themselves into. Sometimes people just end up in there because they've heard something that resonates with them."

"That's true," confirmed Callie. "From what I've read about cults, many people are searching for the truth if they are vulnerable after a death in the family, a divorce or breakup of a relationship. They're trying to find meaning in their life. Not only that but many very intelligent people end up in cults."

"*Really?*" exclaimed Laura. "I find that hard to believe."

"Well, consider this then seeing as how this might be something you can relate to. How many intelligent people do you know of – including celebrities – who've had everything and yet thrown it all away on drugs? How dumb is *that?*" asked Callie.

"Yeh," said Wendy, "or even cigarettes. It may take awhile but they'll catch up to you too and destroy you."

"Well, I don't know if I'd count doing drugs and smoking as the same as being in a cult," said Austin.

"Why not?" asked Callie. "They all have something in common – they're destructive."

"True," conceded Austin.

"So now what are you going to do?" asked Wendy

"Well, whatever it is, it won't be from a basement view," quipped Austin.

"No kidding!" agreed Callie. "You've got your whole life ahead of you. Gotta make every moment count."

"So, what about your parents?" asked Laura.

"Have to wait and see on that. Probably get to visit them. I mean they *are* my parents, after all."

"The authorities aren't going to let them have a chance to do it again," said Callie. "They already showed poor judgment and Future

Life Fellowship in general has been caught in other areas of the state using a heavy hand of authority to get their kids to do whatever they tell them."

"I have to say, though, there's nothing wrong with discipline," said Austin. "I've seen kids like totally out of control where they make faces at their parents behind their back when they're told to do something. And I'm not talking *little* kids either.

"I know," added Wendy. "I've dealt with that personally with the kid I babysit for. She throws tantrums when she doesn't get her own way – at least when it comes to her mother."

"Hey, if you ladies don't have any questions, I'm gonna be heading back home, I guess you'd call it. At least it's not four basement walls."

"Austin, do you really think your dad would've kept you down there for more than a day?" asked Laura in disbelief.

"Yes, I do," he replied, "and here's why. In Future Life Fellowship, and in other organizations like it, obeying orders is held in the highest esteem. I mean people have been kicked out because they've bucked the powers that be. It's just not an option. My dad could have held out longer than I could've and in his mind he felt he had the perfect right to lay down the law and hold it."

"Yeh, but then you're just like a prisoner," said Wendy.

"True, but my job is to obey the authority over me," said Austin. Their view is that God will deal with my father if he's wrong."

"That's just nuts!" declared Callie. "That type of authority is what has young girls ending up getting into a stranger's car because they are told they have to!"

"I know," said Austin sadly. "Thankfully, I don't have an all-out sense of obedience controlling me anymore. I know what things I should be doing, but I've learned to question what doesn't make sense to me."

"Yeh, and to think that's really what's normal for kids our age," said Sarah Jo.

"You know, I actually heard my dad say that if Bishop Jude Bartholomew asked him to hop on one foot and howl at the moon, he'd do it. No questions asked," said Austin.

"You've *got* to be kidding!" yelped Laura as she rolled her eyes incredulously.

"Nope. I'm not. Well, I gotta get going. Nice to have met you, Laura and Wendy. Thanks for asking me to dinner."

"Bye Austin," said Callie and Sarah Jo.

"Yeh, nice meeting you too," said Laura. Wendy waved as he turned to go.

"Nice guy," said Wendy.

"Nice, but kinda weird," added Laura. The rest of the night was spent talking about the future, dating and the Heaven Club, among other things. It was a good way to top off the summer before school began again. Nothing more was mentioned about Austin. Callie supposed their Addison visitors were so shocked by Austin's revelations that they simply had nothing more to say.

CHAPTER TWENTY TWO

History sometimes has a way of repeating itself and that seemed to be the case on this first day of school. Callie was sitting at her computer ready to embark on a new year of studies. Now that she had her career in mind, all she had to do was work toward it. She and her family were very supportive of her choice of being a counselor in an agency which at least had some form of exit counseling for those who'd been in a cult situation. That would probably be easier said than done since the Constitution protects the rights of those who practice freedom of religion. So her form of counseling might be lumped under abuse in one of its many manifestations.

A knock at the door brought her out of her momentary contemplation. As Callie approached the door, she got a sickening feeling in the pit of her stomach. Her hunch was right! It was Mrs. Samuels. She decided to just not answer. Let the woman think she wasn't home.

"Please open your door, Callie. It's Fern Samuels. I've come to apologize. I realize the error of my ways, dear." Callie said nothing and stood frozen still. "I know you're in there. I caught a glimpse of you in the side window."

"Wh-what do you want?" asked Callie haltingly.

"I'd like to apologize face-to-face and beg your forgiveness," pleaded the older woman. Callie hesitated. She would definitely *not* invite her in. She'd learned that lesson well.

"I guess you can meet me out back on the deck," said Callie dubiously.

"Okay. Thank you." Callie wondered on that short trip to the back door why Fern Samuels would be apologetic, especially now. She also knew that it was God's way to not judge before getting all the facts. Callie went out the kitchen door and onto the deck. Just to be polite she asked if Mrs. Samuels might want a glass of water. The older woman declined courteously.

"Please sit down, Callie," invited Mrs. Samuels. Callie decided to sit across from her. She wanted to face her head on so as not to be caught off guard.

"Callie," continued Mrs. Samuels, "as you know we've both been through a trying time, however, nothing like the Reynolds family. They love their son very much just like your parents love you." Callie didn't like that comparison but she said nothing. Mrs. Samuels took that as her cue to go on. "I don't know what you have against us – our church, that is."

"I have a problem with what it does to people, and also that it doesn't follow Scripture," replied Callie.

"How can you say that?" said Mrs. Samuels, her voice getting noticeably louder.

"I'll tell you because you asked, Mrs. Samuels. For one thing, I've never heard of Ambrose before I heard about Future Life Fellowship. The focal point of the Holy Bible is God and Jesus Christ who bought us salvation with His own life. That's the Good News or gospel. Plus, I've never heard of the Alvin Barton Translation of the Bible before I met you."

"Well, maybe God saved the best till last," grinned Mrs. Samuels. That was just *too* weird for Callie. She was about to get up and leave.

"Mrs. Samuels, we have nothing to talk about. You have your beliefs and I have mine," said Callie firmly. "I'd appreciate it if you'd just please leave."

"I'm not done talking and *I'd* appreciate it if you wouldn't rush me," declared the visitor. "You've caused a great deal of trouble to our church, and especially the Reynolds family. Don't think God hasn't noticed."

"I'm sure He has and that's why I'm not asking this time for you to leave - I'm *telling* you to." With that, Callie got up and entered the kitchen and locked the door. Mrs. Samuels sat there looking stunned. Callie ran to get her phone and quickly got a photo of her unwanted guest still sitting on the deck. Convinced that Callie wasn't returning, Mrs. Samuels finally got up and left.

Callie decided to tell her parents about the incident after dinner. She wasn't sure how they'd take it but she knew it was better to keep them informed than withhold things from them. After all, they wanted what was in her best interests.

"You *what?*" asked Dad incredulously.

"Well, she wanted my forgiveness for how she'd treated me," explained Callie.

"She's a known offender!" exclaimed Dad. "I don't mean legally, but you knew what you were getting into when you invited her to the deck to talk."

"Sorry honey," said Mom, "but that doesn't seem too smart to me."

"Mom, we're to forgive. That's what you taught me, and the church did too."

"You could've done that just as well through the front door. No need to make a formal tea out of it," scolded Dad.

"Daa-aad," whined Callie." I did the best I could with her catching me off guard."

"And who is the master of catching us off guard?" asked Dad.

"The enemy – Satan?" offered Callie weakly.

"You got it!" said Dad all too quickly.

*****

"Callie," said Mom. "What's done is done. Let's get these dishes into the dishwasher. Then we'll have dessert. I picked up a pie and some ice cream on the way home from work." Callie was glad for the change of topic and more than happy to clear the table, a chore she usually wasn't eager to do. She thought about the picture she'd taken of Mrs. Samuels that now was stored in her phone. She'd have to delete that image. No point in having it in her phone.

Before going to bed, Sarah Jo called and Mrs. Samuels became the topic of conversation. She half expected Sarah Jo to give her a hard time about being so trusting with her. Instead her friend told her that at least she'd tried. She said that a person never knew when someone might change, especially with help from God.

"I know," said Callie, "but she's so – so set in her ways." She was going to say old but she knew older people, like spouses of church members, who'd changed. It wasn't impossible.

"I think we know that Mrs. Samuels isn't on our side."

"No, she definitely has the cult mentality," confirmed Callie. "I've been reading up on cults and that's the kind of language they use to describe someone like her."

"It's too bad, isn't it? She could be enjoying all that God has to offer. I mean He gave His very best when He gave His Son. How could you *not* trust Him?"

"Easy. When you've been taught to believe and trust in Ambrose. I *still* can't figure out who he is. I asked, but no one could really define him."

"I think maybe he's just a figment of the imagination," said Sarah Jo.

"Poor Austin. Well, at least now he'll get to play basketball – at least if *he* has anything to say about it."

"Yep, the school will be glad to have him on the team."

The next day Callie was surprised to have a visit from Austin, on his way home from school. They too, sat out on the deck but her visitor was quite the opposite of the one from the day before. Austin sat on the glider, his legs supporting his forearms as he looked down to the planks of the deck, deep in thought. In the distance a squirrel scurried about looking for acorns to store up for winter.

"Hey, are you okay, Austin?"

"Yeh sure. I talked to my mother today on the way over here. She called me."

"Really?"

"Well, she's not supposed to be discussing Future Life Fellowship with me, but she did tell me one thing."

"Go on. I mean if you want to."

"Well, she told me she'd talked to Mrs. Samuels and she had told my mother that she wanted nothing to do with you and that she'd kept her distance, hadn't seen you in weeks."

"*Really?* That's what she told your mom?"

"Yep. I told her I didn't really care, except that I didn't want her hassling you."

"Austin, I hate to put it this way, but Fern Samuels is an out and out liar. She came over here just yesterday on the pretext that she wanted to apologize to me. I finally agreed to talk with her out here on the deck, but then she started in on me. So I told her to leave and I went into the house. She eventually left but not before I got this pic of her sitting out here." She handed Austin her phone.

"Wow! What a fake. Supposedly those in the Fellowship are so perfect, and yet she lies?"

"Right?"

"That just reinforces all that I've been through. I'm so glad I'm out of there and in a real church. I have you to thank for that, Callie."

"More like God, I'd say. That was all part of His plan."

"Hey, there's a reason I stopped by here today, Callie." She was puzzled.

"Go on. I'm listening."

"Well, I know you haven't known me too long, but I feel like I've known you forever. What I'm saying is, would you want to be my date for Homecoming?" That caught Callie off guard. She really hadn't thought about public school or its activities, but the invitation sounded interesting.

"Sure, I'd like that," she answered. Austin's face brightened.

"You would? I mean, you would. That's great! It's only a few weeks away."

"I'll be looking forward to it," said Callie.

CHAPTER TWENTY THREE

Autumn became more evident with the passing of the next couple of weeks. Gorgeous fall colors were on the way thanks to the talents of Jack Frost who made his presence known in the early morning. Callie was glad she didn't have to catch a bus or walk to school, especially when the snow would be blowing hard and accumulating. Days like that called for hot cocoa and marshmallows. It was a nice accompaniment to her studying. Speaking of which, she had stepped up her research on cults and the vulnerability of young people to them. It wasn't so much their fault as a matter of just not having a clue. Callie considered herself to be intelligent. Certainly her GPA made that clear. Still, how could she have gotten so drawn into Future Life Fellowship? She wouldn't make excuses but no one had told her anything about the existence of cults right in her own home town. She'd heard of radical ones here and there around the country, but right in one's own back yard?

Callie wondered how many unsuspecting kids were out there, just like she had been, waiting for a cult to set the hook so to speak. Of course, she *did* know that Jesus Christ is the only way to salvation; there was salvation in no other. But others who hadn't been brought up in a Bible-based (not a rewritten "Bible" by some unknown person) church, made a perfect target for a cult. That was a scary thought.

She thought about Austin for a moment. Who would ever have known what a nice guy he was while he was in Future Life Fellowship? He really didn't get the chance to be who he was now – he'd been deprived of that by limiting himself to the confines of that cult. His only real outlet was school and there were restrictions there, thanks to the rules and regulations that he was forced to abide by. But now God was using him, especially through being on the basketball team. From what Austin had told her, the other team members had started asking questions like, "How come you never signed up for basketball sooner?" That was just the beginning, thought Callie. He'd already given his testimony to others, in front of the church. Plus he'd talked to several others who'd noticed the change in him. His life was going to be very exciting and full of opportunities!

That Saturday Callie, and Sarah Jo who'd been asked to Homecoming by Chuck Ladd who was a senior in public high school, decided to go shopping at the Pine Moor Mall. It was small but had all the right kind of stores for a town Pine Moor's size. It hung in there despite SmartMart having come to the area seven years before. The big discount store wouldn't have what Callie was looking for unless she planned to make her own dress. She had to admit that they did have a good selection of fabric and trim.

The girls decided they'd go to *All Things Satin & Lace* and hoped they might see some dresses on sale. Sarah Jo found her dress almost immediately. She knew it was the one. It was seafoam color and featured a sweetheart neckline. Callie's was beige and coral with a dark brown tie belt. It would be just right for the season. Thankfully, she had shoes that would match the belt.

"I'm glad that's over with," declared Sarah Jo. "I mean I like shopping and all but it's hard to find the right dress at the right price."

"I know what you mean," nodded Callie in agreement. They took their purchases and decided to go to Mary's Hometown Restaurant, a couple doors down in the strip mall.

"This has really been fun," said Sarah Jo once they sat down.

"Sure has," said Callie. "I bet kids in cults don't get to do this kind of stuff."

"Prob'ly not. For one thing, they wouldn't be going to a homecoming dance."

"Yeh, and most of their clothes are often homemade," said Callie as she picked up the menu.

"What are you having?" asked Sarah Jo.

"I think I'll have a toasted cheese sandwich. It just sounds good."

"I'm going to have a cup of chicken soup and a turkey sandwich, maybe on rye."

"We're like we've been shopping on Madison Avenue in New York City. Pass the caviar, dahling."

"Callie, you don't sound like you anymore," laughed Sarah Jo.

"I saw it in a movie once," confessed Callie.

"Yeh, and speaking of cults. Kids prob'ly don't get to watch TV. In fact, they prob'ly don't even have a set in their house."

"I know," said Callie. "My dad has said that it takes more character to have a TV set and use it wisely than to just not have one at all."

"Makes sense to me. At our place we do other things. Like on family night we play board games or if it's nice we go outside and do something, even if it's just to go walking."

"Well, my dad wouldn't be without a TV if he could help it. He likes watching football."

"So does my dad. But he only watches one game a week," said Sarah Jo.

"Speaking of sports, I'm so excited for Austin being on the basketball team this year," said Callie. The waitress brought their order and the girls talked between bites. "He may have a career in basketball if he does really well."

"Yeh, wouldn't that be something?"

"He sure deserves it," replied Callie.

*****

A week later found Callie in the process of getting ready for her big date. It was decided, with a little help from Mom and Dad, that she and Austin should double date with Sarah Jo and Chuck. Technically, it wasn't a date but since it had all the earmarks of one, it was considered to be. Not that there was anything wrong with dating. It was just that

Callie's – and for that matter Sarah Jo's – parents liked to keep things casual when it came to going places with young men.

"You've got the whole rest of your life to be with another person. Now's the time to enjoy being on your own. I don't think girls realize what they give up when they become a serious couple with some boy," said Callie's mother when Callie had become a teen. Callie never forgot that and now it made sense to her. Too bad Laura's mother had never told *her* that. There was a whole lot more pressure in Addison to date early, she was sure.

The quartet took in the afternoon football game and the home team won. The crowd was ecstatic. Chuck, who drove Austin and the girls to the game, then took them home to prepare for the dance. They planned to eat out first and then go on to the dance. Sarah Jo had brought her dress to Callie's beforehand, so she would get dressed there. Plus the girls could help one another get ready.

"See you at seven," said Sarah Jo from the front door. Chuck waved and pulled out of the driveway. The girls hurried and before long, they heard Chuck and Austin return. The group decided to go to a nearby restaurant where the food was good and the service equally so. Conversation was no problem even for Austin who was new to dating. Chuck talked to him about being on the basketball team this year and since he was too, he congratulated Austin on making such a decision.

"We need some good players," said Chuck. "Especially someone tall like you. Don't get me wrong though. The other guys are doggone good at their positions."

"I've wanted this for a long time, haven't I, Callie?" Callie nodded. Yes, Austin's dream of playing was put off long enough. The four finished their meals and Austin pulled out his wallet.

"Dinner is on me," said Chuck.

"Then I'll take care of the tip," said Austin.

"Okay, it's a deal."

*****

The gymnasium had been decorated from top to bottom with victory banners and balloons. The school mascot was placed in a prominent area for all to see. This win was a long time coming and the whole community who had rallied behind the team – win or lose – was now seeing the fruits of the team's efforts.

"Would you like to dance?" asked Austin. "I'm not very good but I think I can stay off your shoes."

"That would be appreciated," replied Callie. "My shoes might make it, but it could be hard on my toes." They both chuckled. Sarah Jo and Chuck had taken to the floor among the other couples. Unlike many of those who were out there, Callie and Austin as well as Sarah Jo and Chuck kept a respectable distance between their partners. Neither Callie nor Sarah Jo wanted to give the wrong impression to the guys. It was a big deal to get asked out to Homecoming when not even attending the school. Callie figured it would be a good experience, as did Mom and Dad.

Suddenly, Austin began to act strangely. He craned his head over Callie's left shoulder and as they turned, he looked to the right.

"Austin, what's wrong? Are you feeling okay?"

"I'm not so sure, Callie. Maybe we should sit this one out." That decision was made for them because the music soon stopped. It picked right back up again with a song with a faster tempo. But the couple decided to sit down in chairs placed along the perimeter of the gym. Callie saw Austin look up and over the crowd. A look of dread shrouded his face.

"What *is* it, Austin?"

"Don't look, but you're about to find out." Out of nowhere came two women. One Callie recognized as Mrs. Samuels. The other she took to be Austin's mother.

If she'd had any doubts about that, those doubts would soon be laid to rest.

"So – this is what you do when you account to no one," said the short dumpy one, Austin's mother. Mrs. Samuels' eyes narrowed into slits.

"Shame on you!" she scolded. Callie figured that was mainly aimed at her.

"Mother, don't make a scene," begged Austin.

"Mother? You call me mother now after you turned your father and me in to the authorities?" Her voice dripped with indignation. Callie could see he was fighting to remain strong, but he didn't have much practice dealing with people blinded by their cult beliefs. She hadn't either but she read about it. She'd learned that one must be loving but firm in dealing with them. In this case though, she felt she might only make things worse.

"Callie, why don't you go get some punch or something?" asked Austin desperately. He knew his mother, not to mention Mrs. Samuels, would both be loose cannons and he didn't want Callie exposed to what he saw as his problem. Callie hesitated and finally got up to leave. Immediately, she sought out Sarah Jo who was dancing with Chuck again.

"Sarah Jo, I need to talk to you right away. There's a problem." The three walked to the sidelines where Callie explained what had happened.

"Wow!" said Chuck.

"What should I do?" she asked Sarah Jo.

"I think we'd better bring this matter to one of the chaperones or even Principal Kelly," said Sarah Jo. Callie joined her as she walked over to Miss Grimes, a chaperone. The older woman was watching with fascination one couple dancing a modern dance.

"Miss Grimes," said Callie. "I think we have a problem."

"What dear?" answered Miss Grimes as if coming out of a trance.

"It's Austin Reynolds over there. His mother and her friend from this religious cult is harassing him," said Sarah Jo.

"Religious cult? Why, I don't think I know what you mean."

"I'll explain it to you sometime. We just need for them to go. Austin is in a foster care situation. His mother shouldn't be bothering him," explained Callie.

"Oh dear, let me go find Principal Kelly," replied Miss Grimes, her voice trailing off as she scurried away. As quickly as she'd left, she and the principal returned.

"What's going on?" asked Principal Kelly with a look of grave concern.

"Follow me," said Callie with Sarah Jo in tow. Principal Kelly and Miss Grimes brought up the rear. Callie led them to where Austin and his mother and Mrs. Samuels had been standing. Where were they?

"They must've gone out into the hall," said Sarah Jo. The group hurried out the side door entrance to the hallway.

"I *told* you, Mother. I am almost an adult and, besides, my foster parents know where I am."

"You have only one set of parents," said Mrs. Samuels, "and this is one of them." She gestured toward his mother whose eyes were like two fiery balls of steel in their sockets.

"What's going on here?" demanded Principal Kelly.

"I'll tell you what's going on," said Mrs. Reynolds. "I am this boy's mother and he is going against his father's and my rules." The principal looked confused.

"I don't understand. I think we should take this to my office."

"I'm not in your school here and I don't have to go to your office," said Mrs. Reynolds. "There's nothing to settle. I am Austin's mother."

"I *know* who you are, ma'am," said Principal Kelly. Callie thought the whole situation was surreal. Here these three adults were arguing against the backdrop of Pharrell Williams' *Happy* on the other side of the door.

"You'll know me a whole lot better when I talk to my lawyer about this," said Austin's mother.

"Ladies, please, let's not get hysterical. We haven't even discussed this yet. What do you say we sit down on Monday and hash this whole thing out?"

"I want my son out of here, the meeting notwithstanding," said Mrs. Reynolds. Austin, who had been silent since leaving the gymnasium, spoke up.

"Mother, yes I'm your son. That won't change, and I love you. But the court appointed foster parents for me and you know the reason why."

"You call that a *reason?*" exploded Mrs. Samuels.

"There is no justification for such an outburst," said Principal Kelly. "I'll thank you to keep out of this."

"Well I never!" erupted Mrs. Samuels again.

"Listen ladies, we have a gym full of young people, four of which are right here. I think we owe it to all of them to behave like the adults that we are," said the principal impatiently. "Mrs. Reynolds, if your son was ordered by the court to be in foster care and you disagree with that order, I suggest you go see a lawyer. Otherwise, the law has spoken in regards to his wellbeing. It's not for you, me or, for that matter, even Austin to go against it. It is what it is."

"Well, we look to God as our authority, not the court," declared Mrs. Samuels.

"Ma'am, this is not your business. That is *not* your boy here. So please keep your opinions to yourself," said Principal Kelly.

"I agree with her though," said Mrs. Reynolds.

"I'm going to ask you both to leave. If you care to meet with me during regular school hours, make an appointment with the school secretary."

"Listen," said Mrs. Samuels, "my tax dollars pay for this school. So do Austin's parents. We have every right to be here. We helped pay for this place."

"Ma'am, you refuse to listen to me and I've tried to be patient. Excuse me, while I call the authorities." He walked down the hall a distance and pulled out his cell phone.

"You come with me right now, Austin," said his mother. "I know you can't come back home with me, but we'll go to a cafe and wait until the dance is over. Then you can go back to wherever it is you call home."

"Mother, no, I'm not going. I'm staying here with -"

"The authorities are on their way," said Principal Kelly.

"If I were you two, I'd be on my way before they get here." The two women reluctantly walked toward the outside door. Mrs. Samuels looked back at Callie and gave her the evil eye.

The rest of the evening had been tainted by Mrs. Reynolds and Mrs. Samuels crashing the dance, at least to Callie's way of thinking. Austin was more subdued and even Sarah Jo and Chuck seemed to be putting on a happy face for Austin in particular. Her friend confirmed that later, but neither she nor Callie had any idea of what was yet to come that evening.

When the dance was over, a surprise awaited them outside the school. Parked next to the curb in the shadow of one of the huge maple trees on the boulevard was Austin's parents' vehicle with the window rolled down. The street light revealed his mother who was sitting on the passenger side; his father had driven. Austin pretended not to notice as the four left to go to Chuck's car

"Son, we'd like a chance to speak to you," said his mother. "It's important." Austin did a double take as though he hadn't heard right.

"Austin, you don't have to talk to them if you don't want to," said Chuck. "Just keep walking."

"Her voice sounds different. I think I'll check to see what she wants, but I'll keep my distance. Be right back." Callie figured they wouldn't pull anything, not with the three of them watching.

"What is it, Mother?"

"Austin, I talked to your father about what happened earlier and we both realized how serious this situation has become. We don't want to lose you. We know you're a smart young man. *Something* had to change your mind about Future Life Fellowship. We'd at least like to know your reason for leaving."

"Son, it's all we know. It's what we've been taught," added Mr. Reynolds.

"I – I don't know what to say," confessed Austin.

"There's no need to say anything now," said his mother.

"Just say that you'll keep an open mind about this. If you will, I'll go to Mrs. Hempel and ask if a meeting can be arranged for you, your father and me. We're serious about hearing what you know that we don't know."

"Uhh… I guess so, but under one condition. Don't bring Mrs. Samuels along."

"Austin, I want to tell you what made me reconsider this whole situation. I thought long and hard – and prayed too – as to what I might not be seeing. Then I realized that one factor seemed to always be present – Fern Samuels! I let her do my thinking for me all too often. I'm not blaming her – although she shouldn't have done that. I take responsibility for my part in this."

"I do as well," said Austin's father gruffly. Austin knew it must've been hard for him to admit it, let alone in front of anyone.

"I want to tell you both something," said Austin. "What's happened here has restored my faith in family, that family *is* important. I know God loves our family to bring us to this point of coming to an understanding.

"Your mother and I plan to show you just how important family is – if you'll give us the chance."

"If God is willing to give you a chance then I guess I can too. Oh, one other thing, the basketball team is counting on me. It's non-negotiable."

"That's fine, Austin. We plan to be at your home games," said Mrs. Reynolds.

"That's right, son, and maybe you and I can get in some practice at the park. I used to be pretty good at shooting hoops."

"You got it, Dad!"

*****

Callie was convinced that, indeed, God works in mysterious ways! She'd witnessed it with her own eyes. The fact that God had used her to help another human being come to know Him was amazing. Project Austin accomplished!

The End

ABOUT THE AUTHOR

Barbara Ann's books bring a sense of understanding and guidance for situations that is sometimes difficult for young Christian people to navigate through. Perhaps it was inevitable that Barbara Ann would become a prolific writer and author. An imaginative child, she was transplanted from New Jersey to the northwoods of Wisconsin where Barbara Ann's love of reading and outstanding ability to understand the fine art of wordsmith grew with her, bringing her to a whole new world. Her work as a reporter and editor for her hometown newspaper, brought her even further, lending her the valuable writing process for future endeavors.

Barbara Ann Philleo's Books are available on Amazon.com
Reviews are always welcome

www.ingramcontent.com/pod-product-compliance
Lightning Source LLC
Chambersburg PA
CBHW060924140726
47996CB00001B/365